X TALES
for
0 Minds

Jason Brannon

To order additional copies of this book, contact:
Xlibris
1-888-795-4274
www.Xlibris.com
Orders@Xlibris.com

ISBN: Softcover   978-1-9845-8346-8
         EBook   978-1-9845-8345-1

Print information available on the last page

Rev. date: 06/22/2020

Dear Readers,

To begin, let me THANK YOU for your purchase, and support! You don't realize the appreciation I feel for *all* of you; and I hope you all appreciate the Flash Tales, following this forward.

Next, I need to make *this* very clear:

All stories, characters, and circumstances within are entirely fictitious! If for some reason, you find any relation to the aspects of a certain tale, no matter how minor, I urge you to remember:

"It's only a story."

If you happen to get caught up in the emotion or negativity of these reads, **please** take a step back from whichever one you are taking in, and readjust. Because these horror stories, though short in length, have been known to plunge readers into an uncomfortable misery for certain amounts of time. Myself, included.

I have written these pieces as an outlet from my own senses of depression. And you may find that there is much of that previous pain in each of them. But this is why I am reaching out to you:

So, should ANY of you have this kind of pain, depression, and/or mental distress, you too can get help! Anything as simple as keeping a journal, writing, sketching, getting out and being active, if that is what keeps your mind from wandering into those dark places, then do it! Regardless of the negativity around us, we all have something that makes us happy! We all have something we can do, which allows us an escape from the humdrum routines that we are forced to endure in our adult (or adolescent) lives.

If you don't *feel* like you are capable of using creativity to free yourself, (everyone is capable, by the way) then you can talk to someone: a friend, a confidant, a parent, or even your pets! Anybody with whom you feel comfortable in sharing with or venting to, is helpful to keep your head in the right place. But, say, sometimes it's difficult to discuss it with someone you know; there is help. . . anonymous help, from people who just want you to know that your voice. . . your opinion. . . your life matters. And if you ever feel like the weight of this world is too much for you; feel like you don't have a place in it, anymore, just know

From a friend who understands:

YOU BELONG!

Below is a number you can call, if you just feel like you need a little nudge in the right direction:

NATIONAL SUICIDE PREVENTION LIFELINE: 1 (800) 273-8255

I know things can get tough; and these trials can make you feel low. Nobody likes to feel like their head is being held under the waves, but there is always a lifeline drifting just above you. You just have to find the strength to reach out and grab it! Someone will always be there to reel you in. There *is* help.

So, as I said: these stories can be emotionally draining. If you feel you need to take a break, or skip to another Flash Tale, do it. That one will be there when you are ready to go back to it.

Thank you again!

Sincerely,

With Love,

Jason D. Brannon

His Name Was
Gabriel St. Vincent

"You were a fool, Gabriel." I peered down at the corpse, crumbling onto the street. "Though, as was I. As was I."

In the beginning, I knew this man as only a victim. I had watched him for weeks; for his blood would pump in an atrocious pattern, matched by the wind's arbitrary flow. I'd breathe the scent in deep. Recollecting the feeling of wind. And I'd laugh. To myself, of course. There was nobody else.

This man . . . this . . . fiend, was a brute. Even as long as I have lived. . . existed? As good a term as any, I suppose. Even so long, I have never known of a beast to act towards its own species as this. . . "man". Every week, I followed him. Every other night, he relapsed to his negative demeanor. He was merciless. It did not matter who accompanied . . . or approached. Beggars in the street: he spat in their faces. Women he'd take to bed with him: he bruised them with the "passion" he felt for them that evening. Even his own gang, friends: one night, I witnessed him beat one of his protege to such an unrecognizable mass of flesh, that I heard the suffering's heart stop. For only a moment, however. Then his plasma swam, slowly, unstably, through his veins, once more. This creature, known later unto me as "Gabriel St. Vincent," turned his back to the bleeding, begging, near-dead "friend," and walked.

I've seen cold-hearted. I've seen *heartless*. But until I happened upon this. . . Gabriel. . . I've never, *never* seen anything like him. Thinking back now, had I ever told him this, it might have only gone towards his ego even more. But, this being's blood: hateful but strong, bitter and brutal, I had to taste it. I had to have him. So, one evening, when he was alone, I approached him. He would soon be mine.

The night was uncomfortably warm. Moist. Humid. The gathered storm clouds just outside the limits reeked of piss. Acid rain was swarming into a funnel-cloud two cities over. I could hear the screams. I could hear the news reporters at every corner of the surrounding localities, claiming "this could be the worst storm we've seen in decades." What a pathetic herd of cattle. "Decades?" The Dark Ages, the Plague? Those were fun. This. . . this was child's play. Still, with the coming weather, the screams of the citizens, the smell of urine and the taste of gravel from lack of feeding for a couple hours. . . Yes. . . I wanted to savor this man's

1

blood. I'd have gone the entire month in which I stalked him without eating, if it was possible. Just to make the meal sweeter. Greater. More. . . perfect.

But no. I needed my strength for this one. He hadn't gotten to be the cruelest human being I've come across by being a scrawny fellow. I knew he would put up a fight. Even as cunning as I could be; he was no fool, then. One more whiff of his flesh-coated blood cells, and I appeared.

I was behind him; I mimicked his footsteps perfectly. Light left foot, heavy right heel and toe. Quickening. Stridefully. I chopped my steps in a dance. I knew he was going to hear me. I wanted him to. I wanted him to take me; torture me: as he would his friends. Because, the more I made his veins pop, the more swollen his capillaries, the more perfectly I could dine. He hurried further. He wasn't going anywhere. Ahhh. Reminiscing on that crescent-moon night, now, still feels. . . beautiful. But now I know better. I'll never know another like him. I'll never have another like him. But I rest well knowing, no other creature will, either.

He stopped after only 3 minutes 27 seconds and twelve shuffling feet. I breathed deep as he turned.

"What's your prob--" light bounded from his widened eyes.

VANISH! Everyone knows this trick, by now, I'm sure.

He staggered, slightly, before pivoting back. Now was the most amazing . . . most exhilarating moment of my entire. . . existence. The veins in his neck protruded passed the tendons.

"Wake up, S. V." I heard him mumble to himself before raising his eyes to behold my majestic figure before him. Gabriel was tall, so I had to be just a little taller. I clasped him by the sides of his head, taking in every fast reaction, and reflex as if it was a frame-by-frame projector reel. For splash value, I lengthened my knuckles, so I could interlock them around his head. Or, that's what I made him feel was happening. Just behind his sweating vertebral derm, a street lamp shined like a long-expected dawn. I drew him sideways. I made sure he could see his attacker. I wanted this moment. I had wanted it for seven-hundred, twenty hours. This man was my well-deserved reward. Patience really is a virtue!

As he gazed upon my ever-down-streaming teeth, and my hollowed out irises to take in the night, I felt him begin to pump more intensely. And his adam's apple swelled, the way one does when the tears well in the pits of one's eyes. But the tears were not coming from this one. That hastening of the blood, that swollen jugular, that was his fear evolving. Changing. Into Anger. Wrath. This was the blood I had longed for. I widened my mandible to latch onto that ballooning gullet.

A twang pierced my diaphragm, before I could enjoy his fluid, though. I looked down. Then back up. And smiled. The man had knifed me, just beneath the sternum; lucky me: he missed my heart. I lunged back at his tight throat. And I was right. When I sunk my teeth into his carotid artery, the juice just came in its warm, fast, sweet, bitter, angry, scared, greatness. And, my god, did it come!

I've said this already, and I will forever say it: I had never prior, nor ever after, had a creature such as this. . . Gabriel. Nobody has ever produced, much less projected, as much life-giving liquid, as this man.

But, as they say: all good things must come to an end. He had never been so unpredictable as the moment he turned that blade to my throat, and sliced me. Clear through my trachea. Naturally, I had to release him. Not before, though, my own spray entered his mouth. He lay beneath me, gurgling. Groaning. I stood hunched over him; closing my own wound. Trying not to laugh, so I could heal more quickly. We both silhouetted as blood-drenched shadows against that shimmering, sun-like, street light.

Was the "near-death" experience worth it?

It was.

Was the "new life" I unintentionally gave this cruel beast?

Hell no.

I healed. But the dawn was quickly arriving. What was I to do with this infant abomination? Passed out in the recessing blood and its stains. He had started to heal, as well. I was the fool, that night. I should have just left him there. The sun perches most-admirably over that alley, this time of year. It wouldn't have taken any time at all for this man to crisp like pig fat. I paced around the blood-pool. Mucking up my already stained boots.

"Damn it all!" I thought as I grabbed his collar and dragged him down through the nearest sewer covering. But I wasn't gentle. This bastard *did* slit my throat, mind you. I carried him home. If nothing else, he would serve very well as a blood-sack. I could have chained him up in iron and drained him nightly. An unlimited supply of the most sultry plasma I've ever wanted to feed on. And that's exactly what he was. For about two nights. The ungrateful brute.

After he woke up at about 2 in the afternoon, he tried to speak. He hit syllables, well enough. But the words were only, "AAAAARRRGGGGHHHH!" and "NNNNGGGGGHHHH". Or something to that respect. I saved the fiend. Foolish me. So, I had to keep him alive. Foolish! Foolish Me!!! I fed him my blood from a goblet. His wrists continuously sizzled from the iron. And when he sizzled, he screamed; and when he screamed, his veins popped. And when his veins popped, I felt that urge again! He sweated his last fever that night. And I didn't let a drop hit the stone below. I've never had anyone or any*thing* like him, again. But he was mine now. And nobody would ever have anyone or anything like him, again. Because he was *mine*!

That night, I seduced a young coed and her little sister to come home with me. After all these years, I've found the easiest way to do this is. . .

. . . to be. . . us!

The mortal sensory organs are so naive to the scent, the aura, the flavor, of a renewal of dead tissue, that the signals between those nerves and the brain quickly becomes familiar with it. This is why we "put off" such a pleasing allure. And this is exactly why we must feed as regularly as we do. The longer we go without feeding, the more our flesh, our organs, our fluids begin to ripen. Deteriorate. Decay. And we become the compost masses that Gabriel reduced his "friend" to for such few moments. This is why dead blood is poison to us. Why would we want to ingest what we despise to turn into. It only hastens the process. Anyway, I digress.

My "gifts" for the man fell as wasted fruit, because when we went to him, it seemed he had expired. His blood did stop flowing. His pupils *did* release.

I laughed, "I knew you were an abomination!"

I released his shackling, allowing his body to splat onto the floor. I turned to the hypnotized young ladies and waved my hand. They, too, collapsed to the concrete. I took the younger sister upstairs to feed on. The trouble with the adolescent body: It doesn't contain as much nutrients as a plump and supple college student who eats regularly, but eats well. Red meats. Proteins. Real *real* food. But That was alright, because I had precisely one of those just downstairs.

So, I tossed the girl down into the furnace, and headed right back to get that voluptuous brunette. When I scooped her into my arms, her flesh chilled in bumps like she'd just been jolted by an electric shock. I knew this reaction: she was coming to. But then, that feeling shivered me. I turned. The man wasn't where I left him. I laughed again. Only this time, I had my guard up. Then, that scent hit me again; Gabriel was back from the dead, and standing right behind me.

"Don't do this," I tilted my head in his direction. "You wouldn't know what you're doing anyway."

My voice shook the girl in my arms. She awoke with a squelching cry. She fought to get out of my possession, I wasn't going to fight back. My fight was sizing me up as my back faced him. She ran to the bottom of my stairs before about-facing to see a "hero" in the making.

I joked, "Aw. And she was such a good year."

He retaliated, "I don't give two shits to listen to yours! How do I get out of here?"

"Again, son" I turned, fully towards him, "You do *not* want to do this!"

He stepped at me, "Shut your mouth, goddamn it! You don't know me!"

I lowered my head at his ignorance, "Gabriel." He got still, but not his blood; that was pumping so strongly. It wasn't disappointing.

He didn't want to know. "How the *fuck* do I get out of here?!"

"Such language," I really was offended. In all my life, I've never had anyone swear in my own house! But then again, I've never had anybody like him in my house.

He pulled his knife, again, "Forget it! I'll find my own way!"

"No. Please. Wait." I feigned desperation as he ran passed me. And, as a "good" hero does, he took the coed's arm and led her upstairs. And as a good host, I met them up there. He tried flailing the razor at me again, but I was ready this time. We danced at the top of the stairs. I checked the time: there were only a few minutes before the dawn would crack the sky open, so I let them pass--watching as they scrambled from my hospitable abode.

"Run run as fast as you can!" I called from behind.

They ran. And they ran. The sun rose, more quickly, it seemed, than it had in so long. Then, in the middle of the street, that brutal "hero", Gabriel began to slow. His forehead sizzled as his wrists had in those chains; but this was different. A cherry developed on his brow, quickly rolling into ash. And the ash fell to soot. And the soot enveloped the abomination, leaving his crackling flesh to smoke and fade into the wind. The girl, however, got away with only a second degree burn mark around her forearm. She screamed and ran, and cried and screamed.

But who would believe a story about a vampire abducting her and her baby sister; followed by this guy she'd just met turning into a smoldering statue? Not cops. Not her parents. Not. . . the doctors. So, when they lock her away in that padded cell, I'll be waiting there. Just for her.

From beneath my umbrella, I laughed in the middle of the street,

"You were a fool, Gabriel." I peered down at the corpse, crumbling onto the street. "Though, as was I. As was I."

Leave It To The Clown

"Why are you crying?" asked a rosy cheeked clown to a sobbing little girl.

"I've lost my parents in this big crowd." she replied with a sniffle.

"Oh!" gasped the clown, remaining in character, "well, why don't we go look for 'em?"

The clown reached out for the girl to take his hand. She did with a nod.

"Now, where was the last place you left them, little one?" his shaky voice gave way to the human underneath the paint.

"At the cotton candy booth." cried the girl, pointing just ahead of their present location. "I told my mommy I wanted some cotton candy and she told daddy. So daddy gave me the money and I gave it to the lady. Then she gave me the cotton candy. When I turned around, mommy and daddy were gone! Oh, please, Mr. Clown! You've gotta find my mommy and daddy! Please! Please!"

The clown was taken by the little girl's distress, and led her straight to the cotton candy booth, waving a finger toward the cotton candy lady and smiling as a good clown should.

"Oh, miss!" cried the clown, "Miss? You didn't happen to see where this young lady's mommy and daddy went, did ya?" The clown's voice was squeaky and cheerful, but the girl's cheeks were soaked with tears. The cotton candy lady looked down at the little girl and shook her head.

"No." said the cotton candy lady to the clown, as she leaned from her booth window, "When did you see them last?"

The clown looked back down toward the little girl as she rubbed her red cheeks once again. She spoke,

"It couldn't have been five minutes ago, ma'am." The girl sniffled again.

"And you're sure they were here the last time you were with them?" Asked the clown. The girl nodded. The woman reached back into her booth and pulled out two sticks of cotton candy.

"Well, I sure wish I could help you two," she sighed with unease, "but you can check the 'Lost Parents' office next to the ferris wheel." She handed the cotton candy to the clown and his little lost child,

"Here," she smiled, "two for the road! On the house!"

The clown heeyucked in appreciation and the girl forced a smile. The two turned to make their way to the 'Lost Parents' office. The clown attempted to skip, to lighten the mood for the young one; it didn't help. The little girl wiped her nose with the clown's glove. He shivered with his unsure but goofy laugh, and walked on.

The clown rang the office bell until someone responded. Annoyed, the office worker asked in his least helpful voice: "What can I do for you?"

The clown sneered at the impatient tender before he obliged, "This little girl is lost," he squeaked again, "have you seen her parents?"

The worker rolled his eyes and picked up his ledger. Scrolling through, he asked, "What was your name again, little girl?"

The little girl dropped her hand down to her side and gave him her name.

"That's such a lovely name!" the clown chuckled.

Again, the tender huffed in contempt and fingered his clipboard, almost unwillingly.

"No, child." He said apathetically, "No one is looking for you. Sorry." He shut his window.

The clown was very upset with the office worker's deliberate atrophy. For a moment, he looked away and dropped his bearing. But only for a moment. He then giggled and stated,

"I'm sure someone is looking for you!" He licked his cotton candy in thought. "Well," he said with intent, "what do Mommy and Daddy look like? Then maybe I can look for them with you!" His smile was full of hopeful ignorance.

The little girl began to describe her parents to the helpful harlequin:

"Well," she had just stopped crying to answer his question, "My daddy is real tall! Has a mustache and no hair, so he just wears a silly hat. Mommy is skinny. She doesn't really look forward when she walks. Real small nose. Lots of makeup! Almost as much as you!!"

The clown laughed. And he laughed. He doubled over in laughter. When he calmed down, he put his left foot forward, as to strut, and looked at his new friend, "Well, let's go find them, shall we?"

The little girl, now happier, nodded with a giggle. The two marched, hand-in-hand on through the multiplying crowds. They asked nearly every carney, patron, and police officer they could find. None had had any reports of a missing girl, all day long. The sun was setting. The carnival was just about to shut down. The clown knew he had failed the little girl. So, he took her to the front gate and kneeled in front of her.

"I'm sorry, ma'am." He said in a less cheerful, more human voice. "I don't know where your parents are. But I'll leave you here. That way, if they pass by, you can catch up to them." His make-up had started running from sweat, and it was clouding up his vision. He stood back up, took his glove off, and wiped his face, "I truly am sorry, Little One."

The little girl tugged his pant leg before he walked away and signaled for him to lean back down. He smiled again with a smeared face and stooped to her level.

She whispered in his ear, "I've always hated clowns."

She drew a knife from the cotton candy stick and impaled the clown through his sternum. He fell forward, wheezing in an attempt to moan. He shook violently, eventually folding inward.

The office worker and the cotton candy lady walked up to the little girl. The office worker looked down at the lifeless clown.

"And that, my dear, is how you face your fears." He said.

"Wow, Mommy and Daddy! You were right," the girl giggled, "Clowns really aren't scary, after all!"

Maycontainviruses

So you know how those pop up ads for certain porn websites tend to appear while you're browsing the internet for a good porn website? Who doesn't, right? Well this is about one of those times.

It was a Friday night, and I had a research paper due on Monday. The essay had been assigned on the past Monday to give the class a week to collect resources and to chronicle the facts behind our theses. I hadn't thought about it all week, and Monday was quickly approaching.

Well, I had thought about it…I'd even considered doing it a time or two…but my procrastinative nature withdrew the whole idea from my mental curriculum, and I would entertain myself otherwise. Porn preoccupied my time, most nights. Beer and partying took up the other percentage. As a result, I lost precious acquisition for my research. Not to mention brain cells.

I digress.

I had googled all possible porn sites. Scanned through. Downloaded some vids and bookmarked my favorite URL's. Some pages wouldn't open without clicking "Continue", on the "May Contain Viruses" boxes.

If the address was something really easy to read, it was probably legit. If it was just a bunch of random characters: numbers, letters, etc. I left it alone. Then there were some really interesting titles, like www.doubledogged.com. Or www.trippingtripods.com. They had some seriously messed up sex acts in a few of them. The other sites were just plain-Jane, nothing I had never seen before, pornography.

Oh, yeah! One was actually called "PlainJane.com". And it was about an actual girl, named Jane, who would prostitute herself to any and everybody who paid.

She filmed an introduction "flog" as she called it; it would then cut to her and her suitor beginning their fun. She kept the camera running 24/7, I suppose, only editing the not-so-sexual content out. She had kept her little video black book for a while now, because the very first one was dated back for two years earlier. I grew to appreciate the girl's talent for seducing, not only men, but women, too! What I wouldn't have given for that kind of confidence!

I was just settling in to watch porn…I mean, "write my essay", when one of those annoying pop ups, well, popped up. I exited the advertisement, and pursued my "research". But after about five seconds, another pop up appeared! It looked similar to the first one, but out of impulse and some frustration, I exited out again. I scrolled to see if Jane had any new uploads that I hadn't seen yet. Just as I had found one, the ad popped up again! I was starting to get irate! I was ready to exit out again, but refrained so I could see the title of this persistent invite! The site was called, www.MayContainViruses.sex.

It was easy to read, so I thought it might have been alright; but then I read it again:

www.MayContainViruses.sex

No way! That was too blatant to even consider! First of all, it literally stated that it MAY CONTAIN VIRUSES! And then the suffix, ".sex"? No. I've seen just about all the porn sites' titles and suffixes, and NONE of them read ".sex"! I wasn't going to go anywhere NEAR that site, if I could help it! So, I exited, one last time. Only this time, my whole computer crashed. The screen went yellow, with coded messages crawling in all directions like they were in some sort of word find puzzle! I rebooted my computer immediately.

As soon as the power emblem fell black, I pressed it again to restart. It started normally. No Command Prompt to ask if I wanted it to do so. It just…started normally.

I sighed with a heavy frustration, and simple relief. By this time, I was ready to write my essay! Forget porn! It had gotten me in enough trouble as it was!

So, ready to begin researching my thesis, I stared at the icon screen as it slowly glitched into the desktop format. To my surprise, unfortunately not the good kind of surprise, the pop-up advertisement flashed onto my screen.

With sound, this time.

It was the sound of intense sexual moaning; the pleasure of a hundred different women getting fulfillment out of their personal, orgasmic desires! I exited the box. The screen didn't go yellow, this time. It flashed the ad again. And again. And again. Ultimately, covering the whole computer screen with the ad's erotic temptation. A woman's face was glowing from behind the "click here" button.

No doubt, if I rebooted again, the plaguing site would only be waiting for me to sign back on! There was nothing I could do! Well…there was that…one thing. So I did it. I succumbed to the message's wishes, and clicked the box.

Once I did, the screen cleared. I could see my desktop background again. I dropped my hands in disgust and outrage. The site wanted me to "come" to it, but when I decided I would, it evaporated! What sense does that make?! I grabbed the top of the screen, ready to slam the thing shut; then it flashed again.

The screen illuminated with a hot pink hue, and images and words began appearing on the background. Slowly. Almost as if the "site" was under construction; and someone was writing the code while I watched it build. The first picture was that of the woman's face from the advertisement box. The description was in bits, and foreign characterization. All I could get was, "W ma de p t . M@n m k <3 2 he d." I wasn't sure what to make of it. So I clicked the |> button and waited.

The video, again, glitched into the first scene. It digitized with broken up sound and fluidless movement, so I paused it. Just in case it needed to buffer out. I watched the play bar fill up. Didn't take too long. It was only a 2 minute long video. And after what it had put me through, I didn't want to feel like I wasted my time.

I pressed play again. What I saw on the screen made my stomach clench from deep within my loins.

The video showed a black man with cornrows, a black bandana across his face, and his eyes covered by sunglasses. He walked in front of the screen and raised his shades above his eyebrows like he was taunting whomever dared to watch his vile act…

He then reached out of the camera's view and started pulling it closer to the wall. He turned it to the left, then down, revealing a woman who seemed to be unconscious. He leaned into the camera and signaled the "audience" to be quiet. He started stroking her cheek. He then removed her shirt. I could see she was coming-to. She was dazed, but she noticed the man touching her. He laughed. Or it sounded like a laugh. I couldn't tell. She screamed. The man put his finger to her lips, now. She continued to scream as loud as she could. She attempted to get up and run, but she only collapsed sideways on the floor. It was like she was paralyzed.

She tried crawling as she screamed bloody-murder and sobbed uncontrollably.

The man stood back up. Only his legs and the woman's tortured body were in the shot, now. He lifted his booted foot and began stomping and stamping the woman's back so hard that the camera's audio could pick up the crushing and cracking of bone. He was in no hurry to end the abuse; so, each blunt fracture was slow and painful. The woman's cries and yells had fallen into faint wheezing. She struggled to move. She didn't move another inch. The man sat the woman back against the wall. She was only a mangled blob of bruises now. Suffering with every breath she tried to take. Her eyes looked like they were bulging from their sockets as she adjusted to look at the man who had broken her so. Her face wrinkled with pain.

The man, still standing, rubbed her head then walked out of view. He was back in a matter of seconds, holding something in his left hand, where the camera couldn't see. The woman, unmistakably horrified, began attempting her cries for help, once again. And once again, all that came out were whistles and wheezes. Her eyes dammed up the tears that should have been cascading down her pain-ridden face.

The man jolted forward with an immense thrust of the object in his hand. He sliced through the woman's neck with brutal hatred. He had been holding a machete. The woman's head toppled down her chest as blood, with no time to realize it had stopped flowing, followed, geysing upward in mass gallons. The man had swung the blade so hard that it jammed itself into the wall. He left it and grabbed the severed head by its scalp. He showed it to the camera before he started "making-out" with it.

I had seen enough! I quickly backed out of the page and into the home screen. The date was for a few months prior. I thought it was just some kind of stupid joke, so I didn't bother calling the cops to come out and see it. I scrolled down the page to a more currently dated vid. I should have just left the site altogether!

I found myself zooming past the descriptions that were missing letters or had odd-ball characters to replace words. I made my way down to the bottom of the page. Finally, I saw a familiar face: It was Jane! She looked as disgustingly blissful as ever. Her description was only "<3 Me". Naturally, I clicked on it.

She introduced herself, as she always had, and then she started to describe her newest video.

"Hey guys!" she squealed, "It's me again! I hope you're all buckled in tight, because tonight's thrill ride will be like NOTHING you've ever seen before! That's right! I'm hookin' up and they're bookin' up; so get ready! Get set! Let's have some fun!!"

"They're bookin' up?" I thought. I never understood half the stuff she would say, anyway, so I just continued watching. She brought in her john, and started making out with him as she had with so many others, so many times before. She teased him. Undressed him. He was anxious, I could tell. I would be too. She took some of her sex toys and abused the man in ways one would never disclose among even the closest of friends. She then tied his limbs to each bedpost and started her ritualistic strip show. She gave him such a seductive lap dance, a nun would get "in the mood". The ambiatic music and dim lighting made for a super intense porn scene. Jane finished undressing herself and started "making love" to the man.

After about ten minutes of screwing and moaning, Jane leaned onto the man's chest, put her hand over his mouth and whispered into his ear. She pulled a small gun from the pillowcase, sat back up, pointed it at the man, and before he could get "NO! WAIT!" out of his mouth, she put a bullet into it! Blood splattered onto the headboard, and backlashed onto Jane. She dipped her hand in the plasma and ran over to the camera, gun in hand.

She laughed a sort of sad laugh and rubbed her bloody hand from her cheek, passed her breasts, and on down to her vagina. She lifted it back to her mouth and licked the wet, red, webbing between her fingers. She spoke: "How 'bout this for a sign-off? 'Fuck. You. All.' Isn't this what you wanted?"

She put the gun to her head and pulled the trigger. Her head flung unnaturally sideways. She then fell out of view.

I was almost in tears. I clicked back to the home page. I knew this wasn't a joke. This site was set up for the most heinous acts of mankind! The post date for Jane's last upload was...that day. I guess that's what the description "<3 Me" meant.

Hers was the last porn video I'd watch. With her latest sign-off message being her very own suicide.

I called the police to show them the website. I left the computer on the homepage until they got there; but when I clicked on a video, the site began to glitch. Code was being UNwritten. The site would soon cease to exist. The police laughed it off as I had once tried to do, and told me I shouldn't be watching that kind of stuff. The image cleared, and faded back onto that yellow screen with the coded word find. I restarted my computer again. Only this time, when it booted back up, it went straight to that screen again. It's been that way ever since.

I eventually threw it in the dumpster outside my building.

I have a new laptop now. But just as the first one did, the advertisement for www.maycontainviruses.sex is at the center of the screen. Only...instead of the woman's face behind the "click here" box, all I can see is Jane's still-shot of brain matter leaving her head as the gun goes off. I haven't watched porn since that night. But for some reason...even when my computer is off and unplugged...I feel like SHE is watching me!

The Wreath

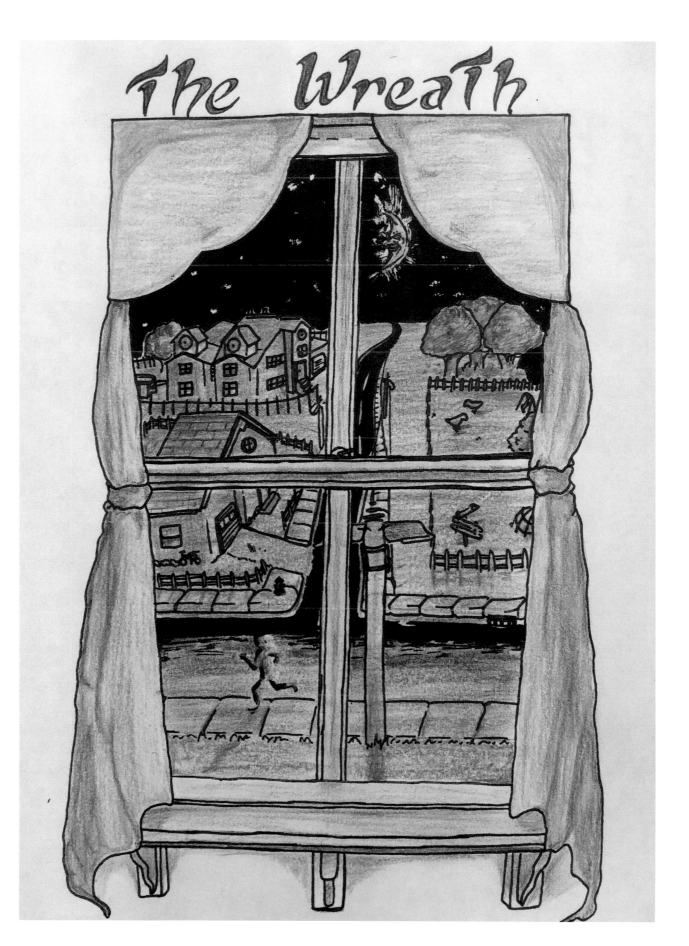

The Wreath

I t was dark when I awoke that morning. A breeze chilled my flesh. I was only asleep for a few hours, I thought. The window wasn't even open. I didn't bother turning on a light; I didn't want to burn my eyes. I strode downstairs to fix myself a much needed cup of coffee, not noticing anything out of the ordinary on my way. I stumbled down halls, assuring myself that I was a fool for not just going back to bed. I hadn't even seen the clock. It didn't matter at that point, anyway. I wasn't falling back asleep. The brightly shining moon illuminated my kitchen. I slithered across the long cold floor, dragging my feet the whole way. I felt my hand touch the surface of the countertop where my coffee pot had once sat.

That's weird, I raised my eyes curiously at the corner. I searched for seconds with my fingertips in an attempt to grasp the old familiar handle. Then I noticed how quiet it was. Disturbingly quiet. Not even a buzz of the refrigerator rang through. Nervously, I fumbled around the kitchen wall to the nearest light switch; I flicked it on...There was NOTHING!

I'VE BEEN ROBBED! I thought with a heavy strain of anxiety rushing over me. All the cabinets, the drawers were empty! EVERYTHING was gone! I ran through the house, making sure I was heard in case the robbers were still in the house, so they would know that I knew. But every light that I turned on revealed empty walls and rooms. Only large furniture was left. I hunted my phone everywhere!

Surely, I thought, I can call the police and get this whole situation under control! I looked and looked, high and low, between cushions, under chairs, even in the fridge. Yes, the fridge! One would be surprised at how often things might end up in the most obscure places. Still, I discovered no phone. And...Before I could close the door completely, I was sickened at another notion. No food. I leaned in with a silent panic. Not frantic as I had been just two moments earlier. Only...unsettled. The interior light never came on. And it was warm. Room warm. It hadn't been recently dismantled. It had been out for hours. Several hours to reach that temperature.

These guys were good, I took in a deep breath. I wasn't even shaking anymore. I was calm as a corpse. Thinking on that expression now seems...humorous. I went into my living room and sat in my recliner.

Hunched inward I wondered, how could that have happened with me just upstairs? So quickly. So...easily. Nonchalant, even. Why?

I thought for a minute longer before realizing there was a possibility that my neighbors may have seen or heard something...Maybe they got hit too! One of them would have a phone for me to use, at least. I didn't even NEED the coffee anymore. I stepped outside. The moisture in the air hung as a crisp autumn morning would...but there was no breeze. It wasn't cold. It wasn't even cool. So where did the chill come from, I wondered.

I walked to my neighbor's house and knocked on the door. No answer. I knocked harder. Still, not even a shuffle out of bed. As loud as I was pounding, I'm sure SOMEONE must have heard. Nobody was coming. I left to try my other neighbor. As I passed my house, I saw the wreath on my door, and the garden was well lit and beautiful this season. I shook my fascination off and hurried over. When I got there, I saw an old woman rocking in her chair on the front porch. I called to her

Ma'am? I called. Ma'am, can you help me?

She just continued to rock. I walked up the steps and knelt beside her.

Excuse me. Ma'am? I repeated. I need to use your phone.

She seemed to be ignoring me.

I pleaded one last time, Ma'am; I need some help. My house was broken into tonight and I need to call the police. Can you help me?

She stopped rocking and turned her head to me.

You're beyond help, son. She laughed in her throat, turned back, and kept rocking.

Senile old bat, I thought. I got up and proceeded to knock on the door.

Someone HAS to answer! They just HAVE to!

I knocked harder and began to explain through the door, hoping to get a response.

Hello? I called out, Can you help me? My house was broken into and I need to use your phone! HELLO? CAN ANYBODY HEAR ME??!!!

I knocked louder and faster...HELLO?! I cried, Will you please just open the door? I really need to use your phone to call the police! HELLO!!

I punched the door with a final sigh of frustration.

Careful, son, the old woman said holding a pink carnation now. She turned to me one more time, You'll wake the dead. She laughed hysterically at herself. I didn't have time for some hags jokes; I knocked ferociously now, repeatedly.

TAP TAP TAP TAP TAP TAP TAPTAPTAPTAPTAP!!!!!

Until finally! The door opened everso slightly. That's all I needed, was for someone to BE THERE!

Thank you SO much, I began; all I need is to use your phone and I'll be gone!

There was no reply.

Excuse me? I opened the door alittle more, Hello? I walked in.

No. I thought. No, that can't be. I stepped in a tad further. No. There's. There's no way. Absolutely. No. NO! I ran across the floor and flung open the curtains to let the moon's light in. It couldn't have been. It was impossible...But...It WAS.

I was back in my room. I was. But I couldn't have been. It was cold, again. But it couldn't have been. Was it?

I wandered back downstairs; everything was still missing. So I ran outside to see if the old lady was still in her rocker. She wasn't. I headed back to my house. And noticed...my garden. It. Wasn't. My garden...Then I looked at the wreath on my door! It...it was...black.

BLACK!? A wave of dread drowned me in an ocean of sorrow as I walked back to the flower bed. It was well-lit by candles. Shining underneath a photo. Several photos. Of. Me. Pink carnations littered the "garden". I collapsed at the shrine. I curled into myself, imagining a rapid heartbeat of uneasiness with six words running around my mind...

"Careful, son. You'll wake the dead."

Pasta Creep

To all who can hear me:

I am your new best friend. I am the one you will cry to when all others have abandoned you. I am the teller of tales: new and ancient. Who am I? I am Pasta Creep!

My first narration is one you have never heard before, I'm sure. It is my own. My rebirth into a thing I had always imagined was only make-believe. My transition into this reincarnation.

It begins, as all good stories do: "On a dark, stormy, night; once upon a time."

I was exactly as you are now. Bored with the hype of new movies, television shows, and worst of all, spoof ghost videos on the Internet! My God, how they drowned me beneath their sick fabrications of the realities of horror! Dismantling the fact behind their so-called "fiction"! I grew nauseated by the constant perversion of facsimilous banter, entitled, "after-dark" narratives. So, I eliminated the spam by shutting off all electronic devices contaminating the air of naturally gut-wrenching intensities. It was pitch black, without the luminous glow of my computer screen invoking its calm ambiatic allure.

What evil would truly lurk in the lonesome darkness which surrounded me? I sat in my hole...silently... for about five minutes. Not in fear, but in curiosity; and it grew stronger by the breath. I spoke. Not knowing why: whether it was to break the insufferable silence, or simply to scare myself out of the comfortable stupor which compelled me to fall asleep. Mentality looming, I expected no response. My gut, however, knotted and pulled at my esophagus with the solitary, unjustified sense that I was not alone.

Of course I'm alone, I told myself. I wasn't convinced.

"Of course you're alone", quoted a faint, almost unnoticeable echo. So faint in fact that I passed it off as being a mental reverberation of my own response. I stood up, feeling around for my lighter...there's really nothing to do in the dark, anyway. I danced around my coffee table, passed the ottoman, right into the fireplace handle. I drummed the mantle, pushing small items about until I felt the single tool I had been searching for. Slapping my fingers on top of it, I picked it up and struck it. FLASH...Didn't light. Struck it again: FLASH...Nothing, still. Third time's a charm, I said aloud. Strike three...the room lit up dimly, so I breathed in deep and let out slowly--careful not to blow out the flame. I proceeded to light the candles on my mantle.

"Heh. Third time was a charm." said the faint, mental echo. It was more distinct this time, but still nothing of concern. The candlelight filled the room in all but the far corner which held a stand-up mirror. I walked toward the corner and struck the lighter: the flame stayed, but no light showed beyond it. I looked into the mirror and waved, my reflection mimicked me. There was no reason for me to be alarmed, but why wasn't there any light in this corner of the room? I extinguished the flame and shook my head. Rolling my eyes, I laughed at my notion of paranormality. DUH! I scoffed, My eyes just haven't adjusted to the light. I sat back down.

I lay my head backward on the couch and closed my eyes.

"WAKE UP!" I convulsed myself out from a peaceful slumber. It was still dark out. My candles had dwindled into teacups with their fires jumping to the tops of each wick, trying not to suffocate beneath their liquified niches. Each one holding onto its oxygen-fed bubbles. They died out, one by one. Only one candle remained on my table: still tall, without flickering; without any sign of struggle or effort to maintain. But... it wasn't my candle. It stood among the dead, wax-plates which still reeked of extinguishing. It was a large, black candle that glowed red from inside; it was otherwise plain. The room was orange from the single source of light. I couldn't make sense of it. As far as I was aware, I was dreaming. I got up to get a closer look at the candle; but just as I did, its flame burst into a greater inferno: renewing and reigniting the other candles on the mantle.

Yup, I said out loud, I'm definitely dreaming. "You must be, right?" that voice rang in the back of my mind, only louder. It chilled me. A silent room, filled with a strained echo and gleaming candlelight. I turned to the corner of the room that held the mirror ; again, it was dark, with only the looking glass shining. Again, I walked towards it. And again: I waved. However, it didn't reciprocate. I cast a reflection. But only merely.

In my counterpart's eyes, I could see the orange glint of the back-lighting candle. The echo spoke again, "You aren't dreaming." My reflection gestured as a marionette, with a bobbing mandible. It's lips followed the words perfectly. I grabbed my jaw. The likeness did not mimic my actions. It sighed. "It's been a while," he chuckled, "hasn't it?"

What did he mean by that? Tried as I might have, I couldn't speak. But it heard my thoughts; and continued a monologued dialogue, "It's been so long since you've gotten away from that false outside world. Where have you been? What have you been doing with your so-called 'life'? I mean, I see you everyday: same old routine. Wake up. Alone, might I add. Get ready for work. Yes. I see you there, too. And," he began pacing with an exasperated fidget, "I always expected that you saw me. You'd lean against the vanity, pressing close against this window: checking your tongue, rubbing your eyes, and then you stare. Deep into mine with thoughts looming, so jumbled...so incomprehensible...with that face. Yes. That face. Until the reality kicks back in and you shove me away to hurry up and wait for your 'life' to begin. Still, you have nothing to hasten your happiness along.

"Seriously, though. The melodrama of television. The antisocial disability of social media. It's all ... so ... depressing!" I knew exactly what he meant by now. I was just thinking about this before I shut it all down. So ... realistically ... I must have been dreaming!

"WAKE UP!" the image jutted right into the silver glass, shouting with ferocity. "IF YOU ARE DREAMING THEN DO SOMETHING! Pinch yourself! Jump out the window! Because, right now, YOU must convince ME!"

I tightened my fingers around a small area of my forearm and squeezed: the pain shot from the outside-in and the burn scattered among my nerves. I still wasn't fooled enough to believe this was real. How could it be? All that ghost talk on the Internet had taught me well enough to not accept just any simple happenstances like this to be true.

"Believe me," the echoing embodiment ceased his fidgeting once again to speak one last time, "if this is a dream, then you will definitely wanna be awake for this. Or," a final pause as he walked out of view, returning with the mysterious candle, in hand. "You may want to be awake before this." He dropped the candle on the carpet and it immediately took to flame, as if it was soaked in gasoline. The blaze hurdled towards my pant legs, while I tried to evade. As it hunted me, I hunted the candle. Stomping each minute inferno as it drew near. The wax peg which started it all was nowhere to be found. The room was all lit, heavily with the heat of my soon-to-be demise. All except that for that one corner. That black hole which held no light. I wondered if it could protect me. The man in the mirror just watched, beguiling. As if he was taunting me to try and escape through the void. I ran as fast as I could into the crevasse, praying for some sort of refuge; but the closer I got, the smaller it became. I slunk back into the mirror's view. The echo was laughing. The heat was rising. The end was imminent.

"Well," said the figure, "it never hurts to try." Suddenly, he burst through the glass, clenching my throat with both hands. "It's time to go!" He shoved me onto the burning table. I was stuck there. The fire slowly, almost torturously, overtook my arms. The blaze weighed me down like an anvil on my chest. I pushed upward with everything I had. The singeing torment was too much to bear. But I had to try. I wanted to, but I couldn't scream. I was already asphyxiating on the smoke that filled my home. But finally, I felt a momentary release. Burning, but mobile, I threw myself onto the couch. Maybe from there I could signal someone for help. Then just as I adjusted myself onto the melting upholstery, I saw that figure from the mirror. "It's time, now, that you become one of those stories that you always swore were just stories." He sat in my place, and we burned together. Mending back into each other, as I had believed we were for the entirety of my existence. Soon, though, the pain was gone.

I awoke later to the smell of burned wood, and the chatter of people. The firefighters had come to save me. But they were too late. My body was crumbling into the couch, and my breath was now a part of the atmosphere. Boy, did I reek, though. My mirror was still shattered. Shards of glass lay everywhere, strewn around the place. It was almost like someone had waded through the debris as it was still engulfed. That dark spot was still in that corner. Still, just luring my curiosity. But, I watched the firemen gather around it.

"Looks like this is where it started," one stated. "So, what're ya thinkin? Electrical?" Another questioned. "I'd have to say so. This guy had a lot of high tech power streaming through these walls." The first replied, "He must have had no life." A third, twisted individual chimed in, "Had more of a life than he has now."

They all laughed.

"Alright," the second voice declared, "let's get him outta here."

They lifted my body onto a gurney. As they walked out, I heard the third voice say, "He had a lotta candles for a dude."

And they disappeared out from earshot.

My place is new again. New residents. New technology. It's really the best way to get around these days. Just ride the wires until I hit a new feed of paranormal inquiries. That's where I pop up. And if you're reading this now; thank you for freeing me. Just don't forget to turn your computer off. And your tv. And your stereo. Otherwise, you may end up like me, one day.

Ha.

Seems, though, you're already off to a good start.

See you soon.

With Love,

Pasta Creep

The Fallen City

The Fallen City

O nce, before the counting of time, set within a beautiful meadow, was a modest, little village. The village was filled with the nicest people anyone could have ever met. There was no crime, no anger, or anything bad within this village.

The village was called Sorna. It's inhabitants were happy and carefree. The children all played as the adults all worked. The elders were respected and commended as founders of the peaceful land. Work was fun for everyone. Men and women coincided as equals. No job was too much or too little for either to appreciate. The people of Sorna were truly happy.

But one evening, strangers rode into the village on giant beasts. The beasts made so much noise as they trotted into the center court. They screamed with a vengeance and smashed some citizens' houses to the ground, with only a flail of the hoof. The people of Sorna didn't know what to do: their homes had been crushed; their beloved village had been invaded! From behind the strangers, trotted a bigger beast than the rest. It was white with horns lining its head and down his neck. Its tail was long and cracked like a whip, from one simple fling. The man upon this beast was even larger and scarier than the beast itself! The man spoke, "Calm down, friends! I do not wish you harm. I only want to help you." The people of Sorna didn't want to believe this man! Who could come into their village, tear down their homes, and proclaim peace? The man continued, "I see your village; I see how my men have ripped it to pieces; and I am sorry! But some things just HAVE to be done! So we can rebuild with greater prosperity!" One citizen cried, "How do you call this helping? We all work so hard to build this village; day-in and day-out! What gives you the right to come to Sorna and destroy it?!" The man replied calmly, "Your tents and huts were not the fruit of hard work, but merely the product of complacency. Hay burns. Clay breaks. Wood sours. Your village was crumbling; it wouldn't have been long before a giant storm came in and washed it all away." A woman retaliated, "They may not have been the strongest structures in the world, but they were ours. They were our elders'. They were our children's! How can you take all that away?" The citizens began to rally. The man was amused by their discontent, and chuckled, "I only mean to give you a bigger, stronger, more fortuitous town. One to be recorded as the greatest city in the world! One, which your elders, your children, and even their children will be proud of. All I ask is that you give me a year! One year, and I will turn this simple village into a flourishing empire!"

22

The citizens, only knowing what they had always known, felt they had no other choice than to agree to the man on the beast. The people of Sorna were all scared for their families' safety. But as the naturally generous inhabitants they were, allowed the men into their village, and even into their homes.

The next day, the man on the giant beast kept to his word. His men began rebuilding the village, using trees from another land and stones from the creek. By the end of the first month, the once villagers were now townsfolk, as their once meak huts were transformed into solid stone houses. The people of Sorna not only had stronger structures to protect them from the weather, but they also had plenty of room in which each family member could rest or play. As time passed, each family would send their children to help the men on the beasts collect materials to build the new city. Some children had the option to stay in the cities from where their materials were collected.

The first year had ended. The men on the beasts had completed their mission to build Sorna to its fullest potential. The citizens were so pleased with the town, when the men on the beasts offered to leave, they begged them to stay. The men agreed. Soon, other outsiders began coming to the town: men, women, children, even more and more beasts were turning up in the middle of Sorna. But as always, the people greeted the strangers with delight; fed them and gave them a place to stay. The strangers were grateful. Most stayed; others were just passing-through. Still, the strangers couldn't all stay with the townspeople without being cramped; this led to much hostility and anger! Met with contempt, the elders and new citizens of Sorna decided that every family NEEDED their own house. So the cycle began. Children old enough were sent out to retrieve building supplies. Every time a new family would arrive with the intention to stay, they would be given a house within the week. This would be the start of the town's downfall.

Years had passed since the strangers first came to the village; and the townsfolk had erected a large castle-like home for the man who started it all! From there, mills for grinding wheat into flour, and farms for raising animals for food were created. Everything was new; everyone was happy; the town was now a city. The city was hospitably dignified. But as the city grew, the foundation beneath was sinking slowly. It was unnoticeable, at first; but once the chickens' eggs began rolling into the center square from all directions, some citizens started to catch on. A scholar from out of town even pointed out the decline to the man on the giant beast; but he only laughed. The scholar decided to go to the general public with his concerns: several followed their leader and laughed. Others felt the dread of losing their beloved city, as well as their families. Few picked up and left.

The city grew every year. The foundation slumped with every new house and building planted within the soil. The city was now a bowing empire; still, people would come from miles around to live in the beautiful city of Sorna. With the people's good nature, nobody (not even the strangers from out of town) could turn a new face or family away.

It had been nearly half a century since the village was destroyed and rebuilt by the men on the beasts. The man on the giant beast was lying in his deathbed as the empire finally sank to its lowest point. The city was now standing in the middle of a giant canyon, surrounded by clay and stone; shrouded in the darkness. Some houses had shattered into its own handbuilt debris. The citizens had wondered why this was happening; the elders knew exactly why. Years and years before, a scholar tried warning of this devastation, and very few had listened. The survivors of the city's descension could not leave the hole their empire had created. Several animals died from the fall. The once beautiful meadow was now barren from lack of sunlight; and too much water from the rain drowned what vegetation was left. The city was dying along with its creator. Yet, even with his last breath, he only laughed. The citizens of Sorna began to starve. War ensued within the once peaceful city. Death befell each family as the months wore through. The empire was destroyed and left desolate within ten years of the famine.

One young citizen who left Sorna, after bringing materials for the houses, came back years later as an old man. He wanted to visit the town he left in what he considered capable hands. He wanted to see the flourishing empire the man on the giant beast had promised; and that so many travelers had talked about. He wanted his soul to dance with happiness with the children and families of his long-loved Sorna! But as he arrived at a cliff where the town once stood, he looked into the hole. A faint glimmer of light reflected from the tip of the flag pole erected on the castle, shown from within the canyon. His eyes filled with tears as he dropped to his knees, ruing the day they allowed the men on the beasts to enter their homes. He knew that his family had died long ago; but the town he called home was now dead along with them. The old man wept, and died on the land he loved a long time ago.

The Bat

Zane, born on August 17, to Daniel and Marissa, was an only child. His father, known to friends as Dan, was a traveling musician. Marissa was a cook at a local diner. Zane stayed with his mother for the first thirteen years of his life because his parents both saw it necessary to keep him grounded: "to not give into the unstable rock and roll lifestyle" as Marissa put it. As hard as it was on the three to be apart, his mother dealt with raising the boy as well as she could on a small-time cook's salary. She'd make ends-meet for about three months and then Dan would come home with a giant check. They'd live it up for a few weeks and after about a month, Dan would leave again. Eventually, the money began lasting longer and longer; because once they'd bought all the necessities, all that was left was what they wanted. Which was never really much. They bought a nice house just inside the city limits, about ten minutes away from the diner. They bought a car. Nothing fancy: just a little scootabout to carry them from one place to the next. Dan bought a travel van for his band, so that when he left town, Marissa and Zane had a way of going to work and school.

Zane was a good student. He did his work and never really bothered anybody. He kept to himself; as he had grown up alone, it's all he'd really known. His mother noticed his estrangement from the other children and she knew it was because of the solitary lifestyle they'd practically forced upon him. Still, she felt she could do nothing. In middle school, Zane met Cameron and Carmen: a pair of twins with just about every difference between them. The three became inseparable. Mainly because Carmen, the younger of the twins developed a slight infatuation with Zane. And Cameron, being the older, held the duty of protecting her with his life. Not to say Cameron wasn't friendly toward Zane, he simply wasn't the "friend-making" sort. After a few weeks of Carmen's following Zane around, her stone-faced twin began to open up as well. And Zane and Cameron became the best of friends.

Fast forward to high school: Zane's dad had been off the road for about two years when he decided he wanted the family all working together,

"I found this great place just outside the limits, Mar!" Dan rushed to tell his wife, who was preparing supper for the three.

"It's this little abandoned shack on top of the hill. Just about twenty minutes out. The road passes right by it and there's nothin' but trees and crop land for miles! We could grow our own food there, Mar! We could

26

start with having the meat delivered in, but after a while we could have our own livestock! Could ya imagine it, Sweety? It'll be a little diner of our own! Just like you used to talk about. Could ya imagine it?"

He squeezed his wife into his chest, which was odd, because Dan was never really the affectionate type; much less excitable.

Zane sat quietly at the table looking on. "Maybe it's haunted," he spoke mild-manneredly as a hinted joke.

Dan's smile decreased slightly, but Marissa's grew:

"Dang it, Zane," she giggled, "you know better than to believe in that kind of thing."

Zane shrugged with a smirk.

"But," she continued to Dan, "I don't know, Danny. I mean, if it's really 'abandoned' then it may take a lot of T-L and C to get somethin' like that up and runnin'. Have you even talked to anyone about it?"

Dan straightened himself up in his serious demeanor, still clasping Mar's shoulders:

"That, I have," he assured her, "I called up to the county to find out who I'd need to talk to in order to purchase the building, as well as the land around it. The lady told me it was the next city's property, but they were getting ready to have an auction for it and a couple other pieces of property around the city. I was hoping we'd all go look at it this weekend; and if you like it, I'll go to the auction next Wednesday. Would you want to do that, Mar?"

Zane sat up with gleaming excitement…or as much as a young grungy teen can get without "damaging his rep". Marissa drew backward and looked up at her husband, his eyes shadowed from the overhead light casting directly over his stern forehead.

"I don't know, Danny," she reiterated, "since you've come off the road, money's been tight. Me makin' what I am…it ain't enough for another set'a bills." She saw the elation flood from his face. She felt her heart shake, as if she had just told him the world was going to end. She gripped her fists and looked down to the ground, "But…" she hesitated, "…if that's what you really want…we'll give it a shot."

Dan tugged her in close again; Zane jumped out of his seat, hitting his head on the low-hanging light fixture and his knee on the underside of the table. Zane laughed it off and sat back down with a more subtle rallying fist thrust into the air.

"STILL…" Marissa concluded, "If I don't like it, we'll just leave it where it stands, right?"

"Of course," Dan replied. "But trust me: you're gonna love it!"

The three, along with Cameron and Carmen, drove out the following Saturday afternoon to look at the location. When they arrived, the structure stood, not simply abandoned but untouched for what looked like decades. The grass was grown up around the sides, as vines overtook the windows and columns across the front porch. A smokestack rested sickly on the cascading tin roof. The area surrounding the building was patched and discolored, for about 30 yards left and right in an almost straight line. Miraculously, though, not a single window was broken.

Dan walked onto the porch to look inside: the door was open. He surveyed the front room before allowing anybody else inside. The interior bore dingy walls and a moldy ceiling. The floors, however, remained fully intact and sturdy. Even as Dan, being a fairly big man, proceeded to jump up and down to test its durability. The old shack included an old basement, which was the most questionable to Marissa. Carmen thought it was the coolest place she had ever been! But that's just Carmen. Cameron and Zane explored the ground floor as the others went below. Every inch of the cabin-like structure was covered in dust, but nothing was beyond use or salvage. It was almost all perfectly preserved from the former tenants. Too perfectly.

The five regrouped and Marissa said the three words Dan was hoping she would:

"I love it!"

Dan chuckled, "I KNEW YA WOULD! Now, all's we gotta do is win the auction, and this baby will be ours, eh, Big Guy?" he threw his arm around Zane's shoulder. Zane nodded.

"But..." again with Mar's stipulations, "...this place is gonna needa get some serious fixin up done before we get settled."

"Of course!" agreed Dan.

"And I ain't doin it by myself, ya know;" she waved her finger as they exited, "you two big strong men will hafta help me with it. Hear me?"

"Yes ma'am," replied Dan...Zane didn't say anything, so Carmen elbowed him in the ribs,

"Yeah. Mom. Duh." he "maintained" his cool guy facade.

"Ooh!" Carmen followed directly after, "Cam and I can so help! Isn't that right, Cam? Huh? Ya gonna help? Right?"

"Um," Cameron replied, "sure. I mean maybe. You know I don't plan that far ahead."

"Yep!" Carmen squeed, "We'll help. No problem!"

Dan won the auction. And within a month, the family, as well as the twins, began renovating the once abandoned shelter. They cleaned the inside, wiping out the mold, dust, and restoring a clean sheen to the walls. What dishes were there, they bleached and washed. the tin roof was replaced with a metal insulated one, and the smokestack was reset and fully functioning. There were preserves and canned foods downstairs. And there was whisky, wine, and blueprints to a moonshine still. Along with the parts piled up in the corner. Dan wasn't much of a drinker, but he had friends who were: so he gave a couple bottles of "the good stuff" to them and kept the rest just in case he wanted to invest in a liquor license for the diner.

Dan built a bunker about an acre away from the shelter itself to store extra food and supplies in case they ran out in the basement. Or so he told Marissa. The real reason was to construct the still for future use. When he told one of his alcoholic friends about the blueprints, his friend reciprocated by stating that his grandfather taught him how to make shine,

"And with Papa's recipe, it'll be a big hit for the bar!"

Dan didn't feel right about lying to Marissa about wanting to sell alcohol, so he told her he thought it would be good for business,

"Widen the margin on our clientele a bit," he claimed. And after weeks of fighting and discussion, Mar gave in and allowed Dan to purchase the right to sell.

"But," again, "the bar has to be in the back, away from my other customers! I don't want some twelve year old getting a beer with his supper. Hear me?"

"Of course, Sweety!" Dan agreed, as he did most of their relationship; but only after he got his way.

Time passed as the diner flourished. But within the walls, since the beginning, strange but subtle events made the family wonder. During the renovation, tools would be laid in one area and end up somewhere completely different in seconds of being placed. Before they opened to the public, as the wine and whisky would be stocked, full bottles would be drained with no evidence of tampering. Doors would open; dishes would fall from the shelves. After welcoming customers, some dinner orders would get ruined from the grill mysteriously increasing its heat. Obviously, these happenstances could be explained by "carelessness, the wind, or simply pranks".

Until one night, after the diner was closed, Zane's family and friends gathered for his fifteenth birthday. As Marissa carried her son's prelit "15" candled cake to the center table, she felt a strong nudge against her back, causing her to stumble forward; nearly dropping the heavily decorated pastry. She realigned herself, shaken but ignorant, and set the cake down in front of Zane.

"Happy Birthday to you! Happy Birthday to you!" his parents and closest friends sang,

"Happy Birthday Dear Za-ane!" the lights swayed and flickered while the candles' flames whisked as well.

"Happy Birthday to you!!"

A strong draft soared through the diner as if the windows were opened all at once. The fire went out; the refrigerator door, oven, and cabinets flew open; and the lights blinked. The front doors swung open and slammed like an angry patron storming away from the restaurant...or rushing into it.

"Well," Cameron stated, "that was...weird."

Zane's parents peered at each other. Carmen, excitable as she is, gave a shiver and ignored what had just happened,

"Yeah, it was;" she concurred, "Oh my gosh! that cake looks ah-may-zing! Can I cut it?"

Her distraction was enough to sway the others into continuing on with their party.

"Um," Marissa replied, "well it is Zane's birthday; and tradition states he gets to cut the first slice, but..."

Zane glanced at the joy in Carmen's eyes, "S'okay, Mom. Go ahead, Carmen."

Carmen squealed, as she often did, picked up the kitchen knife and after a few "ritualistic" spins and swings, liberated the first piece of dessert from its collective confines. She placed it in front of Zane.

"Thanks," he smiled.

She spun the knife between her index fingers, nervously, "Sure! Zane. No problem!"

Cameron was sickened at his sister's obsessive flirtation, "Can we get some too, Sis?"

His naturally carrying voice startled Carmen. So much, in fact, that the tip of the blade penetrated and slid down her finger. She dropped the stainless steel cutlery and immediately squeezed her flesh. Blood ran and dripped from the tip of her digit. It hit the floor like an unsealed faucet.

Marissa gasped, "Oh my! Carmen, darlin'! You alright?!"

"I'll get a rag!" Dan rushed into the kitchen, closing the open drawers and cabinets on the way through.

Zane stood right up and took her finger in his hand; she smiled and tried to speak,

"Don'worry; I'm fi--" she fainted. Cameron caught her and picked her up.

"Oh my goodness!" Marissa repeated, "Is she alright???"

"She's anemic," Cameron then explained as Dan wrapped her finger in an ice cold wet washcloth. "We both are. It's a curse, really. But it's worse for her. . .because she's a girl."

Zane was struck with bewilderment, "Why?"

Cameron cast a "don't play stupid" look at him, "You ever noticed your girlfriend has to take about a week off from school every month?"

"She isn't my girlfriend," Zane laughed nervously.

The others looked at him for a few moments until he picked it up,

"Ohhh..."

"Yeah..." the group shared a moment.

"Take her to the cot in the basement." Dan ordered. They all ran to the already open cellar door.

After applying pressure to her wound for several minutes, Cameron shook his sister to wake her up. She woke to walls of people with faces of relief and her brother holding her in his lap,

"Hey," she smiled, "party over?"

Her brother responded as a brother would, "No, Loser. You passed out and made it all about you; like you always do."

"Aww," she sat up, "I'm sorry."

Marissa defended the young girl, "No, honey. You're absolutely fine. Don't listen to your brother."

"Yeah, Cam," Zane spoke up, "don't be a douchebag."

"Hey!" Dan stepped forward, "watch your language, boy."

"Oh." Zane flinched, "Sorry."

Carmen gasped, "Can we still have cake?!"

Everyone laughed.

"Well yeah!" Marissa said. "But I'll just bring it down here; K?"

"Sounds good, Mom." Zane plopped himself down beside the twins.

Marissa chuckled again, "Well, alright, Birthday Boy."

She went back upstairs; but the lights were all off. She went to the nearest switch and flipped it on. When she looked back onto the dining floor, she saw a restaurant full of people.

"We're closed, guys," she said in a stern but startled voice. "Dan! I thought you locked up out here!"

"I did, Dear!" Dan retorted.

"Well we have a foyer full of customers up here!" she demanded.

"What?" Her husband approached the stairs.

"Come get these people to leave, please!"

"Augh!" he guffed, stressedly, "Alright, Dear! But I'm telling you, I locked the doors!"

Dan ascended begrudgingly.

Marissa never took her eyes off the crowd, who never seemed to notice her until Dan got to the edge of the door. The "customers" then looked at her simultaneously; one wielded the knife to cut the cake.

Dan took one last step, "Alright! Everybody out! We're clos--"

The figures flooded toward Marissa as a giant black mass, pushing the woman into her husband; causing both of them to crash down into the basement. Zane and Cameron stood up abruptly; Cameron accidentally tossing Carmen down as well.

"MOM!" Zane wailed, "DAD! Y'ALL OK?!"

"Yeah," Dan wiggled to stand his bride up after dusting her off, "I'll survive. I reckon."

"So," Cameron helped Marissa back to her feet as Zane grabbed Big Dan, "What happened up there?"

"Your mom--" Dan initiated, "--I mean, 'Ms. Marissa', said there was someone in the diner; so, I went up to shoo them outta here. But when I got inside, Ms. Marissa must have slipped; falling onto me. Isn't that what happened, Mom?"

Marissa was ghost white and shivering. Her eyes, wide like she had just witnessed a traumatic event.

"Mom?" Dan repeated, "Honey? You ok?"

She didn't respond.

"Sweety? Are you hurt?"

Marissa shook again, "No..."

Dan sighed with relief.

"No." she said again. "No. No. No! NO! NonononononononononoNONONONONONONONONO!!!!! That's not what happened!!!"

"Honey?" her husband walked up to her, "what's wrong, Mar? OK, Sweety; tell me what happened."

"They...It. PUSHED me!" Marissa reflected.

"Who pushed you, Sweetheart?" Dan asked sincerely.

"The. The...people! ...? ... But, they weren't... people? They pushed me!"

"Mar, Baby: you aren't making any sense. Nobody pushed you. You tripped. That's all"

"NO!" She defended, "THEY came at me! THEY PUSHED ME!"

"OK, Sweety. 'THEY' pushed you. If they did, then I'll go and find out if 'they' are still here. Find out what they want. OK?" Dan couldn't wrap his head around it, but he was going to give his wife's delusion the benefit of the doubt.

He walked back upstairs; approaching the sill cautiously. He entered the diner. A few chairs were knocked over, and the cake had been prodded at with, presumably "the guests'" fingers. Dan called out, just in case anyone was still in the building. After several moments of no reply, he signalled the other four back up. Carmen was wobbly, but well enough to walk. Zane and Cameron took either of Marissa's arms and helped her up the steps. Once back inside, Zane left the two in order to make sure Carmen got up safe. The five were back in the diner. And nothing, besides a few out of place items, seemed off.

Then, Marissa looked at the wall behind her:

"AAAAHHHHHHHHHOOOOOOOHHHH MY GOD! OH MY GOOOOOOOD!!!" She screamed Holy Terror. She then fell backward, back into her son; pointing and screaming...screaming and crying.

Dan and the others looked to see what had Marissa in such a panic.

It was the kitchen knife. Jammed about 2-1/2 inches into the back wall, just behind where Mar stood, earlier. With icing still clinging to the shimmering silver sides of the blade. Marissa soon blacked out. It was her turn to rest on the cot in the basement.

When she awoke, she left the diner. And never went back.

TO BE CONTINUED...

Past The Woodline

"What was it?!" frantically, I asked my uncle as he came back out from the woodline.

"BIG . . ." he mustered underneath his manic panting.

Uncle Leroy wasn't a young cock anymore. He knew this; but the fact didn't keep him from getting up every morning at 3 A. M. just to catch the day's meals. Some days he'd hunt. Others, he'd fish. Every so often, though, when the freezer was full, and the pantry was stocked, he'd just get up to watch nature.

Before the sunrise, he'd shake my shoulder, "Get up, son;" he'd grunt. "Yer gonna miss it!"

"Miss what?" I'd stir just before I'd roll back over.

". . . everything . . ." Leroy was a man of few words. I know, many people say that about many people. But for him, it was his life.

He wasn't just a hunter and fisherman; he was a woodsman. So silence was his comfort zone. But when he spoke, he aimed to be heard.

We were out camping that evening, when Uncle Leroy, "stepped off to drain the pipe;" he ran back to the fire, stomping it out, kicking dirt onto it. He handed me my canteen, with his finger to his lips,

"Get back to the house, boy." He whispered, the moon shining off his usually patched, silver dead eye.

"Why, Leroy?" I disobeyed, the way a twelve year old boy does in any situation, "What did you see?"

He stayed posed in the quiet position, "Go on, now!"

I turned and followed the trail we made, as swiftly as my feet could scurry.

I heard limbs breaking, and leaves crunching while I ran. My eyes fixated on the glimmer from the cabin-house kitchen window. The noises grew. Echoing my own haste. I heard a shot! I fell to the ground. I still heard the forest floor as it seemed to crack and crumble below. One more shot. . . It was closer. Two sets of clamoring, encroaching footsteps ceased to one set. I lifted my head as the last stopped. Suddenly, I was taken up around the waist, and hustled to the back of the house. The trees blocked my sight from the reflecting moon. I fell from the tuck in his arm when we reached the property line. I panickingly looked back: Uncle Leroy fell onto his backside, in front of me; throwing his breached shotgun down between us. I looked at him from my knees, in the fetal position:

"What was it?!" frantically, I asked my uncle as he came back out from the woodline.

"BIG . . ." he mustered underneath his manic panting. "Let's go make up your room for tonight." he breathed in one last large breath.

33

I nodded. I didn't realize then how much I wanted to, but I learned, *I needed to know* what was in those woods.

"Alright, Big Man," Uncle Leroy pulled the corner of my pillow, "I don't want you going out at night, anymore; got me?"

I nodded again.

"'At's m'boy."

He rose. I pulled at his shirt tail to halt him. He turned.

"Are you goin' huntin' tomorrow, Leroy?" I asked sincerely.

"I'on't know, son." He answered, "Meat locker's run over. Cabinets' still have space to fill, but Auntie is cannin' preserves in the mornin'."

"Okay." I commented in sincerity, "But if you *do* go out, wake me up. OK?"

He pulled his shirt gently from my hand, and walked to the door. He looked back, slightly, and nodded.

I woke up at 9 A. M. the next morning to the lines squeaking as Auntie pulled the clothes from them. I ran downstairs. The kettle was moments away from screaming at her. I sat at the table, waiting for her to come in and Leroy to come down.

She walked in the back door, laundry in hand, "Good morning, Sleepyhead." She called with a smile. "Breakfast is in the oven. Done got cold, but it's still good."

I walked to the stove and got the remnants of sausage, eggs and biscuits.

"Y'all done ate?" I asked.

"Yeah, baby." She responded, "I waited for your uncle, but he didn't make it back in time."

"Back? From where?" I questioned before snapping into my sausage, egg biscuit.

"You know, 'from where', son." she laughed, "He went huntin' this mornin'. A lot earlier than usual, though. That's why I thought he might've been back sooner. Guess th'old fool fell asleep in the woods again. Poor man. He doesn't get the rest he needs. I try tellin' him, 'Old Man, you're fixin' to have to let someone else to the huntin' and fishin' 'round here.'"

She went on and on, as she always did. My only thoughts were about last night: What *did* Uncle see that made him go back into those woods?

I ate what I could before excusing myself from the table. I ran back upstairs to get dressed. I sneaked into Uncle's room and got his six-shooter from behind their headboard. I stuffed it down in the small of my back, where my belt would hold it, and my shirt would cover it. I was going to find my uncle. And I was going to bring him home.

I headed out, and surely enough, Auntie was canning preserves when I left.

"I'm goin' out, Auntie!" I hollered.

"That's fine, baby! You don't wander too far; but if you run into your uncle, send him straight home, y'hear?!"

"Yes ma'am!" I replied, backing towards the woods.

As soon as the hill blocked my view from their back porch, I turned and rushed the trail we made the day before. I made it to the campsite, but the fire hadn't been relit. I did, however, smell smoke. I plundered the still standing tent for a rifle for long-range, if I *had* to use it. There wasn't one. I followed the smell of burning brush; not new; not extinguished; but burning just long enough to distinctify. There were broken limbs, chopped roots, and flags hung from trees. Uncle Leroy had definitely taken this trail. I shuffled through the forest with high hopes of finding Leroy with a sixteen point buck, or a slew of eight pound catfish! Anything that he may have just had too much of, and couldn't carry back home, himself. I did find him. He was in a clearing. And he *was* at a pond. He lay on his side; dead eye roaming as his good eye remained half-shut. His upper-body was drenched. His jaw wrenched. As if he was gasping for air, but also like he was confused. He couldn't speak. Not sure that he would, if he could, though.

I used all of my preteen angst to lift and drag Uncle Leroy back away from the water. I didn't get him far, but I did manage to pull his torso away from the shore. His clothes were torn in odd places. But not like a bear or wolf or *any kind* of animal would do. I looked around for Leroy's rifle and shotgun; the shotgun was in the fire, still breached but empty. I didn't find the rifle.

"Uncle!" I tapped his cheeks, hopeful for some comprehensible description, "What was it?! Was it what you saw last night?"

He writhed.

"Was it a bear?!" I continued my interrogation. He shook his head. "Was it a coyote? A gator? What!?"

He grabbed my side and leaned forward, "It . . . was . . ." he gulped with an expression of anguish, ". . . The Yeti!"

I found this to be very, *very*, odd. And even harder to believe. I tore open Leroy's shirt to check for abrasions. All I found was a giant bruise circumventing his left side, around his ribcage. His ribs were broken. Still, the shock had him feeling bearly much of nothing. There wasn't anything I could do for him, except let him rest. But at that moment, my goal was to find the beast which almost killed my uncle, and return the favor.

I started to rise, revolver in my hand. Uncle grabbed me again, "Go home! Get Auntie!"

I nodded.

He shut his eyes and I headed back into the woods, to find the creature. I looked for tracks, broken limbs, tufts of hair, blood, if my uncle shot it. I hopped, ran, and swam, for about three miles before I came across a cave. A looming scent of charring meat and hair emanated from inside. Whimpering faintly accompanied it. There was spottings of blood leading directly into it. This had to be the "Big Foot's" hideout.

I didn't have a torch, or a flashlight. How was I going to approach it? There seemed to be a fire inside, but for how long after I entered? I took a stone, as big as my hand, back then, and tossed it. I heard it hit the floor, bounce, and slide. A grunt followed. I hear a shuffle of bipeds coming to the entrance. I could have counted the moments that struck me as it got closer. My heart raced. My blood boiled and my face burned. In a second, I remembered my gun. . . I raised it. I shook.

A pale, bare, bloody leg emerged from the cave. A furry arm showed soon after. And eventually, the head of . . . a . . . man? He was pale. Pale-*green*, just about. The furry arm, was a fox coat, crudely crafted. Handmade by the "monster" himself? His legs were covered in old, tattered bed sheets, it looked like. His face was scarred, with what appeared to be metal covering his skull. Rusted around the edges. His neck was scarred, too, with frayed stitches; some still intact, others, just hanging there. His arms were long, muscular, and veiny. Juggernautish. He held his left side as he exited. He growled. He groaned. He staggered closer, but fell.

"Who-" I asked in my rattled voice, "Who are you?" I waved my gun, not sure if I expected a response.

"AAUUURRRGGGHHH!" He responded, retaliating by waving his branch-like arm at me.

"Y-you better answer me! Or I'll shoot you dead!"

"Shoot," the man groaned, "shoot *me?!*" he seemed offended. "*You* are on *my* doorstep! You have no justification, here!"

Shocked at the answer, I took half a step forward, "You hurt my uncle! I see he got you too! I come to finish the job!"

"Your *uncle*," he spoke groggily, "was in my woods! I was only after food. He assumed I was after *him!* HE ATTACKED ME!"

He looked at me, and the sun showed an old withered face, with grey sunk in cheeks and dark like eyes.

I stepped another half further, "N-no," I trembled my gun, "We were campin' last night. We weren't after no trouble! And these are *his* woods, mister! *You* have no business here!"

"I," he started to stand back up, shoving the dead animal off his shoulders, "have been here longer than any other man, boy! This is *my* home!"

He reached his peak, and he stood, gigantic.

My jaw dropped, simultaneously with my gun-wielding hand. But my speech was not hindered, "My great-granddaddy built that cabin before his wife died fifty years ago! Can't be older than that house; no sir!"

He chuckled, then fell again, slightly, "I have been in these woods for one-hundred, twenty-four years. Ever since *my* father died."

"You ain't pullin' nobody's leg, 'round here, mister. I wasn't born yesterday!"

"It doesn't matter," he cried. "Shoot me, if you want! I grow tired of being alone. I didn't want to hurt your uncle; but he gave me no choice. But *you* have that choice, now, boy!"

I shook my head at the request.

"This is your only chance, boy! KILL ME!" He lunged at me.

I turned and ran the other way. I heard his cry and groans distancing behind me. I made it back to Leroy, and used all my might to lift him onto my shoulders. I don't remember what happened to my gun. We raced to the house. Auntie dropped her preserves and shrieked.

"Help!" I screamed, "He needs help!"

Auntie loaded Uncle up, and took him to the doctor. Just as I suspected, his ribs were broken. He spent a week in the hospital. When he was well enough, I told him about the man in the cave.

"And he told me," I laughed nervously, "'I've been in these woods for one-hundred, twenty-four years,' Hahaha!" I hoped for a reassuring response, "Isn't that ridiculous!?"

Uncle grunted. "Auntie," he looked at his wife before answering me, "'one-hundred, twenty-four years,' i'nt that around the time great-great-pappy said the old Frankenstein castle burned down?"

She nodded, "Why, yessir, Leroy! I surely do think that's right!"

Nobody Dies In This Story

First of all, let me just say:

Nobody dies in this story. So, you can feel a little better about that. It's really just a story about a family. A mother. A father. And their three beautiful children.

The eldest is thirteen; she pretty much takes care of the other two. She's such a sweetheart. One wouldn't believe she's really as young as she is. So mature.

The middle child is nine years old. She isn't able to get around too well. She was born with leukemia; she's never been able to know her true hair color. She doesn't mind, though: she has a rainbow of wigs she gets to decide between before going out with her family. Mostly, though, are "bad days." She can't even get out of bed, sometimes. What-with all the IV's and machinery. Her older sister has to take care of her, those days.

Still, the youngest is about three. He is just a bouncy, lovable. . . healthy. . . baby boy. He's. . . so. . . happy. *All the time!*

It literally is a sight to see these three amazing young'nes together. The way the eldest looks after both of them is uncanny. It's beautiful!

Their mother: she, herself, is a remarkable creature. Superbly bewildering. Running around the house, making sure everything is perfect for the family. No dirty dishes. No dirty laundry. No stinky trash littering their immaculate home. No blemishes of any kind to make the abode look any less. . . than perfect.

Then there's their father: Always working! Ensuring financial stability for his steadily growing family. He never allows them to go hungry. Never lets the bills stack up. Never even hesitates when he has to work extra, every once in a while. He isn't typical. . . He mans up when it's time to show everyone else who's boss.

Or that's how he tells it.

Every night, as "father" comes home, he is greeted at the door by his wife with a loving kiss. She then shows him to the dining room where his plate is ready with the hot meal she just finished preparing for her family. "Mother" calls down the kids. The eldest carries down her waddling baby brother, and straps him into his high chair, before rushing back up to help her ailing sister down. The five sit at the table before saying grace.

"How was your day?" Mother asks Father before he groans in contempt.

"Bad?" she follows, "Maybe supper will make you feel better."

"Yeah," Father replies, "because it's *not* exactly what you fix *every DAMN week!*"

"I'm sorry, Love." She puts her fork down and dabs her lips, "I thought you liked it."

"Not *every DAMN week*, I don't!" he suggests, "Listen, I provide more than enough for you to buy for more than ONE kind of meal every week!" Why not try switching it up a little? Y'know? Like *pork chops!* Or *STEAK!* Can't go wrong with a good steak every once in a while, I tell ya."

Not wanting to start an argument in front of their children, she bows her head, "Yes, darling."

Halfway through dinner, the middle, sickly, child vomits. It's a shame. This was the first solid meal she's had since she got back out of the hospital, two weeks ago. Out of reflex, her father throws his fork down: he's disgusted. He doesn't mean to be. But he is.

Her mother rushes towards her with a towel and a glass of water.

Her sister moves their plates so neither is sullied further by the young girl's. . . accident.

Her baby brother just watches. Unaware that any of this is abnormal. This is all he has ever known. He giggles. Such a sweet sound. One of which goes unnoticed by the others.

Later on, the children are in their bedrooms, and their parents are talking amongst themselves.

"Darling," mother begins, "I didn't want to bring it up in front of the kids, but you know with the doctor and hospital bills piling up, we can't afford to buy that kind of food!"

"Yeah, yeah yeah," rebuttals the father, "We've discussed this all before."

"Then why insist upon bringing it up every month?!" She feels the war has to start somewhere.

He fires back, "Because, MAYBE I would just like us to enjoy something we don't get to every so often!"

"But this is all we can do, *right now*, you ungrateful piece of--"

"--'piece of what, you wino bitch?!"

"You know 'what'!" her eyes bulging and welling with tears.

"Right." he remains seated in front of the glowing screen, just twisting his head slightly towards her. "So, we can't afford a nice cut of beef, but you can afford to get tipsy with your girlfriends, from time to time. Stay classy."

"You know it helps me cope. Just like that whore helps you!"

"Yeah. Whatever."

"So, *you admit it!*"

The voices are only muffled by a pillow over the elder sister's ears.

The middle sister lays in bed with a half-drank bottle of vitamin milk on her night stand. She's still awake, aware of everything her parents are saying.

The baby cries. And is ignored. And he is ignored until he cries himself to sleep.

The next morning, the girls come down for breakfast. The baby is already eating and their father has already left for work. "Mother" stumbles at the sink while the smoke alarm goes off. The bacon is burning. And the toaster is in the dishwater. Fortunately, it's unplugged.

The three year old, not liking the noise, wails while covering his ears.

The eldest opens the back door and kitchen windows to wave the smoke out. And throw out the bacon.

"Okay, girls," their half-drunken mother chuckles, "off to school!"

It's summer vacation. The children are out of school. So, they simply take their brother for a stroll. It's a "good day," for the sick sister. She can walk. She can smile. She can forget that she is sick.

And then she can't.

After a couple hours at the park, the three finally make it back home. The alarm is no longer screaming, but their mother isn't to be found. Conscious, anyway. As unusual as it is for the kids to see "mother" drunk and incapacitated, they feel it isn't anything to concern themselves with. The girls put the boy to bed for a nap, before the elder helps the younger to her own.

The eldest sibling heads back downstairs and watches tv. About an hour before her dad gets home, she tries waking her mom. Her mother is drooling and bumbling like a junkie after a hit. So, she starts supper, herself.

When her father gets home, he completely ignores his dozing wife, as he makes his way to to kitchen,

"Something smells. . ." he stops in dismay, ". . . Where's your mother?"

"Oh," she excuses, "she's resting. Said something about not being able to sleep last night. It's fine, Dad." She smiles. "It's almost ready."

Her father walks back into the living room and snatches her mother up by her arm. She's obviously startled from her stupor.

"What is wrong with you?" She demands.

"I should ask *you* the same thing!" he snarls. "Why in the world is our daughter slaving in the kitchen? Huh? Tell me THAT!"

"I don't know!" she responds, "Maybe she's learning how to be responsible."

"It's because your drunk ass is passed out on the sofa! *THAT'S why!*"

"I was not passed out! I'm not even DRUNK! It's just been a long, exhausting day and I needed a rest!" She pulls her arm from his clasp.

"You need a sponsor, is what you need!"

"Dad!" their daughter calls, "It's alright! I don't mind. *At all!*"

He replies, "Yeah. Well, I *do*!" He pushes his wife into the kitchen, "Now, sit down. Eat your supper! We'll discuss this tonight!"

"Mother," rests her head in the crease of her elbow, on the table, while the others dine. "Father," disgustedly gazes at the seemingly lifeless body of his bride.

This goes on every week. Day-in. Day-out.

Eventually, "Mother" has to go to anonymous classes; to rid herself of her "dependent disease."

"Father," begins seeing his mistress more frequently.

This leaves the children alone more and more.

The eldest still makes sure her siblings are fed and taken care of; having no time to herself.

The middle child is maintaining. She still can't eat real food. And she still can't brush her real hair. But she believes she feels better.

The baby. . . gets fed. . . cleaned. . . takes naps. He's happy. Not the "happy" you and I would know, but the "happy" he has only ever known. One day, he might look back at his dysfunctional family and wonder how any of them survived. How any of them managed to smile every day.

Maybe he'll never have to wonder. . . Why nobody dies in this story. . .

The Raid

The Raid

The lights went out during the raid. The whole city was in trouble because of it. No one was safe. The night owl gangs were running amok. The police were off dabbling in whatever mischief could pay more: i.e. turning their heads away from the true crime which plagued this god-forsaken village of a town. But if the drugs or violence didn't pay the right price, the police were all back on the side of justice. Hell. Sometimes "the side of justice" is only left up to the criminals. What a way to live, huh?

I pulled my family away from the doors and windows, in case some crazed gang affiliate or cop decided to bust into my house. We went into the cellar via a trap door in the hall. It wouldn't be noticed by anyone in the dark unless they knew it was there. The serrations matched the lines in the floor perfectly. The only difference was the finger hole drilled into the opening side to lift the plank. My wife and I shuffled the kids down as quickly as their tiny feet could flee.

My wife followed. Before I descended, myself, I gave a quick glance at the window in my youngest son's room. A mooncast shadow whisked by. I hurried down to rejoin my family, pad-locking the door behind me. Once below, I signaled for everyone to huddle together, and to stay as silent as possible until the raid was over. We held each other for about 3 minutes before we heard some rustling on the concrete behind us. A paint can twanged and skidded away from the corner as two distinct footsteps adjusted themselves into an upright standing position. The basement window caught some rays from the low-hanging moon, outside. And I caught a peripheral view of the silhouette of an intruder in my home!

I side-stepped in front of my family, pushing them back toward the stairs trying to maintain their silence. I reached onto one of the shelves that contained all of my worktools, keepsakes, etc. in an attempt to grab a flashlight. I didn't look at the shelf; my vision was fixed on the fiend in the corner...he didn't move. Whether he was malevolent or just a bum who wandered into our basement window when everything went down, I didn't know. I didn't care. All I wanted was for my family to be safe. And it was up to me to assure them that I would be their savior.

After some knocking and tinkering for a flashlight, I finally grasped a cylindrical object; I picked it up and started fumbling around, searching for the "on" switch. When I couldn't find one, I broke the line of sight between me and the invader to hold the object up to the window's light. I was holding my oldest son's model airplane we had gotten him for his ninth birthday. He was excited about it when he opened it; he just never got around to gluing the wings on. I'm never getting him a model ANYTHING ever again.

42

I turned to my family and told them to crouch within the shadow next to the staircase. I grabbed the crowbar, that I knew was on its own rack at the bottom of the stairs. I quietly approached the motionless man, whose eyes gleamed with his own personal fears. The closer I got to him, the stronger the scent of grime and trash grew. I knew at this point, he was definitely a vagrant.

"What are you doing down here?!" I asked in a violent whisper. He said nothing. I raised the crowbar to scare the man. It worked. He shuttered inward.

Still, he said nothing.

"I'll give you till the count of three to get out of here. Then I'm going to kill you myself!" I threatened with only a quarter intention of following through. I began counting.

"One…" he stood, only whimpering. "Two…" he pushed his arm up toward the window. "Two-and-a-half…" he had to know I was bluffing by now. But by the time I reached three, just his feet were left inside. The smell of fish and garbage remained. As he crawled out, voices surrounded him, as did the shadows of God-knows how many figures. I backed out of the light and listened.

"Over here, boys!" a voice chortled. "Looky. Looky. What have we got here?"

The voices ceased. Followed by the sound of pounding and crunching. Pinging of metal bats. Thumping of tire irons. Spelunking of knives all entering and leaving the man's body. He kicked violently, suffering! Until…he stopped struggling. I pulled back even more.

The last thing I heard from the voice was: "Hey, man. Gimme that saw." Then there was that sickening sound of a rubber band being cut through by a dull knife, into a block of wood.

Blood drained from the grass into the window. I ran over to my wife and kids. Fortunately, they had only heard the muffled voices. The feet were dragged through the window, and the light was blanketed by something oblong and bushy. I cuddled my family closely.

After the ruckus settled down. My family and I stayed huddled. My wife started humming lullabies in her frozen, shaky throat. My kids, wet-cheeked from fear, nodded off. I kissed my wife's forehead and leaned her against my chest. She fell asleep soon after. I tried to keep myself awake for the duration of the night. It was to no avail. I slept until dawn. Final gunshots and squealing of tires woke me.

The sun breached the obstructed window, and I got up to watch that which I had dreaded might never come: daybreak. I pulled myself away from my family to remove the rock or whatever it was stuffed in front of the window. The nearer I got to the window, I saw that it was open. The thing wasn't sat in front of the window, it was pushed into the window. Now, I smelled rotting fish. I tiptoed closer. I now realized: that thing blocking my view, last night, was no rock or brush or anything of nature. It was…the hobo's head!

Party People

I don't celebrate my birthday, anymore. Not because I feel like I'm too old and have grown out of it, or anything. But because the last one I had a party for. . . I almost didn't survive.

I was eleven. Just old enough to know exactly what I wanted but not nearly old enough to know. . . ha ha. . . exactly *what* I wanted! Like I said: I was eleven; and my birthday was only two days away. I had been planning for weeks how I wanted my birthday to go!

I was really into pirates that year. Why? I'm not exactly sure. The idea of independence and just living among the waves, in search of buried and sunken treasure thrilled me! Having a subordinate crew beneath me. . . was always. . . I don't know. I always appreciated a chain of command; be it in the military, movies about gangs, and especially pirates! Pirates had their own laws. Had their own plans. Let nobody tell them what to do.

Maybe that was the reason I liked them so much.

You see? I was a push-around kid. At school, I took so much crap off from EVERYBODY. There wasn't any difference between the students and the faculty, either.

I tried to tell my parents about it, time and time again. But among their work schedules and. . . whatever it was grown ups did back then. . . wine parties, maybe? They were away from the house all the time. But they left me in good hands. My big brother. He didn't ignore me. But we were in two completely different schools, so he couldn't help me when I needed, either. He just dropped me off in the morning and picked me up in the afternoon. When we got home, though, it was *always* about me; I mean, after homework.

I do not miss homework.

So, two days before my birthday party, my big bro asks,

"Did mom and dad ever order your party stuff?"

I shrugged. He had a look of confusion on his face,

"Come on, dude. How can you *not* know?!"

I looked at him and said the first thing that came to mind,

"I haven't seen either one of them in, like, a week. I doubt they even know my birthday is coming up!"

He leaned in, lightly punching my arm,

"Don't say that." he laughed, "OK. I'll find out. What did you want? Pirates?"

45

I stared with half-shut eyes at my brother, in half disbelief and half non belief that he couldn't remember. Then I looked around my room. He followed to notice all the pirate "memorabilia" covering my walls. With the exception of my calendar, which had birthday reminders, all within a foot and a half of it; marking the day when I would finally be. . . twelve!

"Got it." he chuckled, removing himself from my bed.

"I got it." he repeated leaving the room completely.

The phone was just inside the kitchen, which was just outside my room. I heard the receiver lift, followed by the singular speed dial button being pressed. . . I listened,

"Hi, is Pat around?"

. . .

"Yeah. It's her son."

. . .

he sighed, "yeah. The oldest one."

. . .

. . .

. . .

"Hey! Mom!" he became aware of his volume; lowering his voice, ". . . hey. . . did you get Bruce's party scheduled? . . ."

. . . .

". . . you're kidding, right?. . ."

. . .

". . . seriously?. . . how could you forget your son's birthday is this week?. . .

. . . .

". . . no, mom. . . it's fine. . ."

. . .

". . . ok. . . yeah. I'll call dad. . . maybe he was more helpful than you are. . ."

. . .

He hung up the phone with a bit of agitation.

He dialed the next speed call button.

He followed with a sequence of button mashing. Dad worked in an office, so he had an extension line.

. . .

"Yeah! Dad!"

. . .

"Dad. . . it's me. . . who else would call you 'Dad'?"

. . .

". . . yeah. . . not funny. . ." he started talking quietly again.

Almost like he knew my parents were failures.

Thinking back on it, maybe I should be more respectful.

". . . hey. . . you ever order Bruce's party stuff? . . ."

. . .

". . . no. . . Dad. . . you're just as useless as mom. . ."

SLAM! He threw the phone down, harder this time.

"Bruce?" he called from down the hall.

I waited a few moments, then stepped out,

"Yeah?" I tried to say without letting my chin quiver too much.

"Hey!" he seemed super excited, "Hey! Mom and Dad ordered it about a week and a half ago! They just need me to call and confirm it!"

I smiled. I knew he was lying. I heard everything he said prior to hanging up the phone. So. . . I smiled.

I headed back toward mom and dad's room,

"Hey," he called from behind me, "Where ya goin'?"

"Um. . ." I thought real quick, ". . . I gotta pee!"

I looked back at him and he nodded, turning back to the phone.

I rushed to their room, closed the door, slowly; and picked up their phone. Just in time, too:

"Th-th-th-thanks for c-c-calling 'Party People's': where our d-d-d-dr-dream is to m-make yours c-c-c-come t-t-true!" the voice was of a teen about my bro's age.

"What w-w-wish c-c-c-can I gr-gr-g. . ." he sighed, and tried again.

"Wh-what wish c-c-can I grant y-y-you today?"

"Tom?!" my brother recognized the voice. . . or maybe the stutter. "You work at Party People?"

The voice laughed, with heavy anxiety,

"Y-y-y-yeah! M-my folks o-o-o-own it. Who-who-o is this?"

"Hey, man! It's Sonny! From school!"

"Oh-Oh, y-y-yeah! H-hey, dude! What's up?"

"Hey, my little bro is turning twelve in a couple days. And my retarded parents forgot to set something up. Do y'all have pirate stuff?"

I could hear the roomy echo in the phone. I wondered if he could hear it too. If so, he never said anything.

The voice hummed,

"P-p-pirates?"

My brother repeated,

"Yeah. 'Pirates'."

"W-w-w-we have J-Johnny Depp stuff."

"Nah-ha-ha!" Sonny laughed sarcastically, "Wait. . . Really?"

"Y-yeah! Just like. . . w-wait-wait. No. Ju-just a c-c-c-cardb-board c-c-cut out."

. . .

"Y-yeah! We-we-we ha-ave p-p-pirates! Do you w-want just cha-cha-characters, c-c-cake, or th-th-the c-c-combo?"

"Send all ya got!"

"O-O-OK! How-how will y-y-you be p-paying for this to-to-to-today?"

"Credit card."

I sneaked out of the room while he was reading the card number off to the guy.

I was so happy! But I had to contain it from fear that my brother would know that I knew!

The next two days dragged by.

But when my birthday came, I couldn't have been more excited! My mom and dad were both there. I know, that doesn't sound like something I should HAVE to say. They tried, that day, too. Mom made me a cake and Dad was blowing up balloons. They didn't float. Maybe I was just ungrateful. Maybe they deserved it. But, at least they did try. Because it was my birthday…? …because they didn't have to work…? Maybe both.

Sonny kept staring at the clock. My parents didn't seem to notice too much, but I did. It was 11:05 when the doorbell rang. The "friends" that were going to come had already made it about an hour earlier. There weren't many. So their parents stuck around for the entertainment to arrive. And at 11:05, they arrived.

Dressed in gnarly pirate costumes, it was a group of five. The Captain strode in, first. Swinging his throat-cut over the heads of the parents. Then laying it over his shoulder, marching, eyeballing my guests. Next were the first mate and two buccaneers waving and popping off the plastic bang guns, kicking their knees high in the air. Finally, and for some reason, there was. . . a mermaid. Decked out from her shimmering tail, to the seashell bikini. But, she was *no* Little Mermaid. She was just as dirty and rank as the pirates! Still, true to character, she squirmed on her hands through the doorway. The pirates "yo-hoed," and "arr-harred" all the way through the living room,

"Where be the salty birthday dog?!" The Captain growled.

He pulled out his pop gun, shiny as a real one, and spun in place. The room shuddered with solitary giggles from parents. The children were a little frightened, myself, included. Which is why I was slightly apprehensive when they called for me.

"Arrgh!" claimed the First Mate, "When the Captain asks ee question, he deserves an answer!"

The parents still laughed. Mine shoved me to the Captain.

"Ah!" he gleamed, "Ye be the scoundrel! What's the matter? Catfish got yer tongue?"

The mood was...heavy. These guys were really into their roles. Then, the Mermaid approached me. She started to sing,

"Happy Birthday, to you

Happy Birthday, to you

Happy Birthday, ye scallywag"

CLICK! I heard the front door lock. One of the pirates twisted the deadbolt...

Odd, I thought...

"Happy Birthday, to. . ."

BANG!

I fell. My chest felt like it was collapsing. I heard screaming and watched through fuzzy eyes as the other kids scrambled. The parents didn't move much. Until the Mermaid drew a small knife from her waist and stabbed one of them in the throat!

BANG! BANG! CHING! POW!

Flashes and cries surrounded me as I faded.

I woke up several days later in the hospital. I could hardly breathe. And my chest remained heavy. Nobody was around, until the nurse came in. She called for the doctor as soon as she realized I was awake. I couldn't speak. I could hardly hear.

I wasn't cognitive enough to make anything out. I stayed groggy, and unable to be awake too long. It wasn't until I was able to get out of bed that anyone explained what happened. And why nobody was there with me.

"Do you remember what happened, son?" the doctor stood at my side, not looking up from his clipboard but every so often.

I shook my head. After trying to speak; but words hurt.

He put his board down and with a sigh, began:

"A few weeks ago, at your home, you were shot by an escaped convict. Your mother, your father and brother, along with a few more of your house guests sustained gunshot and knife wounds. Three of your friends did not survive. Only one of their fathers walked out of the house, with little to no injuries. He was an off-duty police officer. Fortunately, they carry their weapons all the time. But two children, not including yourself, are stable. Only three adults survived. Sadly, your mother, your father, or your brother, did not. I'm sorry, son."

I shut down. And fell back out of consciousness.

From the day I left the hospital, I was placed in a foster home. A lot of the time, it felt like my real home. . . Always being ignored and forgotten. Unless somebody needed to blame me for something. Then, I was the center of attention. I only missed my brother. He was the only variable between that life and this one.

I never spoke to anyone about why I was put in that place.

Those "pirates" were all escapees from the state prison which was located just one county over. Serendipitously, for them, the Party People's van was heading to my house as they met the road. They were all killed by the cop at my party. It wasn't until they were dead could he get back to his car and radio for help.

Well. . . I'm 20, now. I don't celebrate my birthday, anymore. Usually, I just take the pills and sleep it away. I hope after every dose that it will be my last. Then, maybe, I can celebrate my birthday with my brother. But. . . As the years pass. . . I'm beginning to think the doctor is giving me placebos. I just go to sleep. I. . . just. . . don't want to wake up, anymore! Maybe this dose will do it. . .

Happy Birthday, Dear Scallywag. . . Happy Birthday. . .

Painted Expressions

My brother died when he was twelve. I was fifteen; and I was supposed to *always* look out for him. I failed my role, that day.

He had soccer practice one afternoon, and I would usually go with him and dad: earning my title as "Big Brother." But I had a new girlfriend. You know how it is with teenagers! All I wanted to do was spend time with her, plan our "happily ever after," together, and make out. Unfortunately, on this particularly rainy evening, our happily ever after would end with my little brother Tim's life.

Like I said: Tim and Dad were heading over to the practice field, in our broken-down, little scootabout with nearly bald tires, (it's a wonder Tim ever got to play sports, considering how broke we were) and they were already running late. Typical. My brother was always a little whiny when it came to everything he wanted. But he was the baby. So, he got a pass. Not around me, though; he knew if he wanted my attention, he would have to be a soldier. A gung-ho, balls to the wall, trooper! When he was with me...he learned tough love.

Well, according to Dad, Tim was complaining about how late they were,

"We're not gonna get there 'til everyone else is gone, Da-yud!" he would imitate in that prepubescent Tim voice.

Well, "Da-yud" looked back to fuss at my kid brother. As he looked back, they were fast-approaching a red light. Dad slammed on brakes. The tires slid, hydroplaning to the middle of the intersection. Another car was zooming on, "trying to avoid getting caught by the light," my dad would recall. I guess the other light was yellow. That's my only justification. But, I wasn't there, so.

The car rammed the rear passenger-side of my dad's ride.

"He never seemed to slow down!" Dad cried.

Tim's body...looked like it had been run through a trash compactor. When the police brought me and my mom for. . . confirmation. Dad was in the hospital with three broken ribs, two fractured, shattered hip and arm. He suffered some internal as well as external bleeding. And a slight case of whiplash. So...he couldn't exactly make it to the funeral.

The driver of the other car survived the crash. He resided in the same hospital, on a completely different floor. Intensive Care Unit. The asshole wasn't going anywhere fast now. Except, maybe Hell.

A few weeks after the funeral, after fasting over my failings as "Big Brother", I began hallucinating. I'd see Tim in the hallway, at my bedroom door, in the middle of the night. He wasn't abandoned model clay, anymore though. He was just. . . Tim.

A lot of times, I'd see him so clearly, that I would forget about the accident. I'd forget he had ever left; I'd ask him, "What's up, buddy?" or "Tim? What's wrong, man?"

Because, every night, when I'd see him, he'd have a somber expression across his face. It almost seemed like it was painted on. The dimension and detail was there; there was simply *no* emotion.

Some nights, I'd get up and walk towards him. As my eyes adjusted to the light . . . or dark, he would disappear. It was just like in the movies. It was creepy as hell. Then, some nights, when I approached the apparition, he vanished; but it felt more like a dream.

"Maybe you were sleepwalking. . ." my mother would suggest between muffled sobs.

I tried explaining to them, that he's been coming to me almost every night for the past few weeks.

"Listen," they'd sit down with me, "we *know* this has been hard on you! It's been hard for all of us. You aren't the only one who misses him, you know."

I stopped talking to them after a while. Isn't it just like parents to make a shitty situation even shittier?

"Whatever," was my new catchphrase. Or, at least, that was when I started using it, like every other brooding teenager.

I began waiting up for my brother to show. I wasn't exactly sure if it worked like that, but I *literally* had nothing to lose. My parents didn't believe me. I had left my girlfriend after the wreck. I abandoned my friends. So. Fuck 'em.

Surely enough, though, just as I was sitting awake in my room, anticipating the arrival of my unforgotten sibling. . . he didn't. I sat there. I watched the doorway. I looked at the clock: 1:16 AM. This was typically the time I'd awaken to my brother's presence. But he was AWOL. But what did I do? I waited longer!

1:30 AM: Nothing.

2:00 AM: Nada

2:45 AM: Absolutely, not a goddamned trace!

"Maybe I am just crazy," I thought to myself. Still. . . I stayed awake.

3:17 AM: Eyes got heavy.

I didn't care. It wasn't like I *needed* to go to school the next day, anyway. I would just sleep in.

3:18 AM: I was gone. My mental will was not stronger than my physical urge to rest. But I realized. . . that was alright.

3:19 AM: There he was. Standing at the threshold to my bedroom.

His painted expression glitched. This was new. Different. Unsettling.

"Spence." His lips didn't move. But it was his voice; and his. . . expression. . . glitched. . .

I wanted to speak. I even tried. It hadn't been this difficult before. But to hear his voice. . . coming from *his* being. . . just sort of caught me off guard.

"H-hey, Tim!" I was shocked that that just blurted out. But have you ever thought about something so hard, that it just jumped out of your mouth? That's what that was, I think.

"Hey, Spence." He giggled. Still, with a voiding veil throughout his visage.

"What-" I stammered, "What have you… you been up to?"

He moved. Forward. Yet, he never *moved*; if that makes sense. Probably not.

Whatever.

His nearly whole body showed grey and blue with the light from my window. The back of him lit up more vividly, but more distortedly, from the hall's luminescence. It was almost like he was reflecting the glow from behind him. . . like a camouflage. His face glitched, again: only this time I could see a smile pixelate from it. It sounds weird, I know. But if I came out and said "he was holographic," then it wouldn't even come close to being accurate! So, imagine him as one of those articulating, wooden models; then picture someone putting highly detailed decal-sticker of a face: eyes, nose, mouth, moles: everything so perfect about him, and it being completely imperfect! But. . . his voice. . . and now his smile. . . this *was* my little brother! This was Tim!

"You don't have to be afraid of me," his voice soothed the air with a brisk low tone. "It's just me." He shifted, motionlessly, again. His smile blanked itself away.

"No, Tim." I assured him, "I'm-I'm not *afraid* of you!" I laughed nervously, "You know me: I don't get scared."

I stood up, cautiously. I wanted to run to him! I wanted to hug him! But. . . he disappeared the last few times. . . I didn't want to have to wait a whole 24 hours before I could see him again. Granted, I *was* legitimately scared out of my senses. But I couldn't let him see that. I shambled, exhaustedly towards him, still at yield. And as I drew in, his. . . existence became more hollow. More transparent. The blues and greys turned into more of a reflective primer; until I made it right to him. When I got in front of him, he was gone.

I stumbled to my knees, into the doorway. I pounded the carpet with my fist, just knowing I screwed up! No matter how many times I let him get away from me, I was still so selfish that I tried it one more time just so I could hold him! I regretted this, mostly, because I never took the opportunity to embrace him when he *was* alive. I resented myself, because I failed him when it mattered!

I buried my face into the shag, in an attempt to dry my silent tears and choking gasps.

"Big Brothers don't cry," I'd tell Tim when I got scolded for whatever I might have screwed up, or even when I broke my leg playing football.

"Big Brothers don't cry," I repeated to myself, trying to stand back up.

I walked to my bed with wet cheeks, but was halted. . . by the blues. . . and greys. . . and reflective primer in the form of an articulating mannequin sitting, back against the wall in the center of my bed. I was halted. And I remained there,

"You're-" I gulped down the dissolving lump in my throat, "You're back!"

His glitchy image was all but new to me, now. I watched the sides of his face extend, in such a frame-by-frame motion, I was almost sickened. But as it manifested into that Little Brother Smile, I couldn't help but feel a sleepy sense of calm immediately after.

"I didn't go anywhere," he giggled again.

I sat on the floor.

"Why do you keep coming to me, Tim?" I asked with a shutter, realizing how cold I must have seemed. Especially when his head glitched slightly to the left, mouth, partially opened, and eyes glimmering widely in the faint light.

"I mean," I corrected myself, "No matter how many times I tell mom and dad that I see you, they never even try to believe me! Why don't you go show them *you're real!?*"

He vaguely shook his camouflaged head "I can't go to them. They don't want to see me."

"What do you mean, kid? Of course, they do!"

"No, they don't!" he raised his voice. I heard him do this, plenty, when he was alive. There was *no* doubt in my mind that this was my Baby Brother.

"OK! OK, buddy. Then keep your voice down," I chuckled, shaken.

"What is it, pal?" I asked, standing back up, "What do you want me to do?"

"I don't know," he began to whimper, "I don't know why I'm still here."

"Well, there has to be some reason, Timmy."

I began walking towards him again, "If I come sit with you, you're not gonna disappear again, are ya?" I tried to laugh to settle my nerves. Maybe it would help him feel better, too.

He shook his head.

I made it to the bed, and looking at that bending light through my grey, little brother, I felt sick again. My body...my mind...knew this wasn't natural.

"This isn't normal," I guess I breathed aloud.

"I know." He sniffled.

I sat beside him and looked into those electric eyes as they glowed downward. I leaned against the window above my bed, and just watched him. We didn't talk, much more. We just sat there; and we were at peace.

The same thing happened the following nights: we said "hi", and enjoyed each others' company. I was satisfied with that. Then, the more we stayed together, the more he began to look more like himself. He moved more fluidly. . . there were no more pixels or glitching. I almost forgot his disposition. I would occasionally ask if he'd ever figured out why he was still around, and he'd just shrug. I know it doesn't sound it, but I thought it was kind of polite. What's the etiquette to talking with ghosts? I don't think that was one of my high school extracurriculars!

One night, though, I asked him, "So, what are you still doing here?"

And he said something I never expected to come from his mouth, "They said. . ." he hesitated for so long, ". . . I need somebody to come with me."

The hair on my arms stood on end, but I laughed, "What are you even talking about, kid?"

"They said I can't go with them until somebody comes with me!"

"OK! OK! Calm down, buddy! Who said that?"

"The Soul Keepers," he looked at me with his bright eyes, now dimmed with distress. "Who else?"

"I'm sorry, Tim," I stared at him with a smirk, "I don't have friends like you do."

He nodded. "Yeah. The Soul Keepers told me I need to take more people with me:

'Think of it like a carnival ride,' they said, 'the operators can't start the ride if there aren't enough riders!'

"They were weird!"

I laughed again, then inquired, "Oh! OK! So, you just have to wait for more 'riders' to join you; well, I'm sure several people have 'cashed in their tickets' by now. Don't you think that would be enough?"

He shook his lowered head, again, "No. It's got to be certain 'riders'. People who were supposed to 'get on' when I did. The people who are responsible for my 'riding'."

I couldn't laugh anymore.

"And who are those people supposed to be?" I asked.

He looked at me, "You know who they are."

Then just like that, he was gone. Again!

But now, my head was full of names of "the people responsible" for my little brother's death. And I knew all of them.

The Driver of the car who hit them.

My dad for not paying attention.

My ex-girlfriend who kept me from being there for Tim.

I didn't see Tim again for a week. Well, I didn't see him until I went to see the driver of the other car, at the hospital. He had recovered well enough to be moved to a real room, a couple of weeks, prior. I remembered his name. I got his information. I went to see him in his room.

I had picked up a complimentary ink pen out of the lobby. I knew this would be messy, but I had to do it. I *had* to clear my brother's list.

He slept. Almost. . . peacefully.

"Are you kidding?!" I thought to myself, as I watched his chest crest and cleft, like the murderous waves of the rippling ocean.

"How can you sleep, knowing you took the life from a twelve year old boy?!"

I ejected the pen, and moved right next to the evil slumberer. I hovered it over his swelling jugular. Then lightly placed it onto the dimple in his neck. I lost the patience to hesitate, and thrust it into his neck. As the sharp pain startled the bastard awake, I grabbed the pillow from behind him and shoved it over his face. This drove the writing utensil deeper, and absorbed the blood as he suffocated. I kept the pressure over his face until his monitor flat-lined. I rushed out of the room shortly after. I knew I would get caught, soon; but not until I finished off Tim's fellow 'Riders'.

I swept myself to my ex's house, and text her to come outside. She did, and I took her for a walk. We went to the park, the whole time, I ignored her questions of why I was so sweaty. And if that was my blood. And if I was ok. And blah blah blah!

I pulled her behind a tree and kissed her. Grabbing her by the sides of her head, as if to give her the most passionate and soul-burning arousal a teenage girl would ever experience. As I pulled away, her head still in my hands, I looked into her amorous eyes. They were brown and gleaming. Her smile reflected her affection. . . I pushed her skull into the tree. Her eyes rolled, senselessly around her now swollen sockets. Her face turned purple from the sporadic rush of blood to the front. I smashed her against the trunk again. And again. And again! She must have bitten her tongue at some point, because the last time her cranium hit the bark, a mass of flesh jumped onto my face. My knuckles had started to bleed from scraping the wood. I didn't care. I sat her down onto the roots, and kissed her puffy, bleeding, blue lips.

I ran home.

My dad rolled himself into his bedroom in his wheelchair, only to find me sitting on the edge of his bed. I held his .38 special revolver in my hand.

"What are you doing in here?" he demanded.

I raised myself up with the gun pointed, eagerly at his chest. He raised his good hand.

"Son," he began to bargain, "put that thing down. It's loaded."

He maintained a sort of calm demeanor as the muzzle poked the buttons on his shirt. I don't understand how. At this point, I would have been pissing all over myself; squalling, *begging* for my life. But not him. What the hell kind of monster isn't even afraid that his son is pointing his fully loaded six-shooter directly at his heart. He didn't deserve an explanation. . . Even though he asked,

"What's going on? I know Tim's death has been difficult, but *please!* Put it…"

I shot the gimp. Blew him backward about a foot. No. He didn't die. He just stared at me. In awe, I suppose. He must not have felt it. So, I pressed the heated barrel to his wound, and watched him writhe. For a few moments, he understood exactly what the "ticket to ride" really costs! His eyes drooped closed. And his head fell. The expression of agony still. . . painted across his face.

My brother appeared right next to him, with that beautiful and innocent smile that I missed for so long! He walked, not glitched, up to me, and touched my leg.

"Big Brother?" he requested.

"What is it, buddy?" I smiled with a tear.

"There's still one more responsible. And one seat left." He giggled.

I looked down at my sweet baby brother, "I know, Tim. I know."

I put the gun beneath my chin and pulled the trigger.

…BLACKNESS…

I didn't see a carnival. I didn't see the other "riders". I only saw Tim.

He glitched. And spoke. But it wasn't his voice. The glitch wasn't the same. It was like he was stuck. . . like he couldn't respond. He was. . . taller. His face. . . didn't hold the same "painted expression." It showed like a television screen, with Tim riding a carnival ride. With my dad. Behind them were my ex and the other Driver. They were already excited to get the ride going!

The screen closed-up to My Little Brother. He said, "Thank You, Big Brother."

I teared up. The screen went black. As did the room. Then, I saw lights. Carnival lights. And they spelled out.

"WELCOME TO HELL: Have your tickets ready"

Mommy Tucks Me In Every Night

I luv my mommy! She's the sweetest mommy in the hole entire world! Dady doesn't no this but she gived me all the tootsy rols out of the Halloween candy. Tootsy rolls are my favret! She always gives me hugs and kisses befor I go too bed. Then she stil coms in and tucks me in. And she gives me kisses then to!

But I bin sad a wile. Mommy didn't com tuck me in all elevinty too days last week! Dady told me that he had to go tuck mommy in every day. I had to sta with my baby sitr every day to. I hayt my babysittr! She don't do nuthin but wach teevve. I didn't get a snak all day one day!

She's so meen!

But that's ok. Mommy was back at home tooday! I don't had too stay with the meen uld baby sittr no more.

But mommy is diffrint! She was meen to dady all day! And she didn't look at me to much nether! I hop mommy is ok. I hop she not mad bekas I cuddnt com tuck her in wif dady. Dady told me I can't, mommy! I swer! I wanted too com tuck u in wif dady and give u kisses to! But I had too sta with that meen old baby siterr!

Don't bee mad mommy! I'm soree.

I won't lett dady tel me I can't com tuck u in no more. I'll com tuck u in if you want me too. And give you kisses to.

Mommy?

Is that u? It is u! Mommy I'm so hapee! I'm sory I cuddnt tuck u in mommy! U're not mad at me ar u mommy?

"No, sweetie. Mommy's not mad at you. I'm going to tuck you in tonight. Don't worry about Daddy and me. But...I want to tell you something. I can't tuck you in after tonight."

Why not mommy? I wnt u too tuck me in! I'm not to big yet!

"I know, darling. But mommy is...mommy has to go away for a while. But Daddy will take good care of you! I promise!"

But dady is always werking mommy! Pleese don't go away! Pleese! I promiz I won't bee bad evr agin mommy! Pleese don't leve!

"Sweetheart...you're gonna make mommy cry. No, baby. It isn't anything you've done! Its nothing anyone has done! I...just have to leave. I'm going to such a nice place though! It's never cold and I can watch you all the time! I can keep you safe where I'm going. But you have to do something for me..."

Wut mommy?

"Tell Daddy I love him. Give him kisses everyday. Tuck him in every night. Tell him, Mommy's made her trip safely..."

But were are u going mommy? Does dady know where u're going? Y were u meen too me tooday? Wuts rong mommy?

"Yes, baby. Daddy knows where mommy went. When you get old enough, he'll tell you everything you need to know. But that's all I can say right now. I Love You, Sweetheart. Mommy Loves You."

Wait! Can I hav wun more kiss tonight? Seeins as u can't tuck me in no more...

"Of course, my love."

Thank you, Mommy. I Love You too!

"Now, hurry! Go tuck Daddy in! He needs those hugs and kisses, right now."

Yes Mommy.

Dady? Where's mommy going? Y...y are u crying?

"Oh, no, son. Daddy isn't crying. Daddy's just sleepy. And mommy just stepped out for a minute, Baby Boy. You'll see her in the morning"

No I won't! Mommy sed I won't.

"When did mommy say that?"

Wen she cam to tuck me in tonight.

"No, son. Mommy stepped out a few hours ago. She hasn't been back."

Nuh uh! I seed her 10 secunds ago! In my room! She sed too tel u she maid her trip saflee.

"Her trip?"

She sed u noo she was going on a trip! And wen I git old enuff, u'd tel me all about it. Oh! And too giv u bunches ov kisses and hugs and too tuck u in evry nite!

"Son? Mommy couldn't have told you all of that..."

She DID!! I swer!

"Come to Daddy, son. Sit beside me."

Ok dady.

"Listen to me: Mommy's trip...was...to Heaven. And she went a couple days ago. So she couldn't have talked to you."

Ef she left a cupple days ago, who was that lady in the house erleer? She lukd like mommy.

"That was your aunt, son. She came to get a few of mommy's things that mommy wanted her to have. They were twins, you see? They had the same birthday. And they looked a lot alike. You won't see her too much though. It's just gonna be me and you for a while, Sport."

Oh. Wel that lady wasn't hoo was in my room. It was mommy! I swer!

"I believe you, pal. Because, even though she isn't here, she can still-"

Keep me safe. I no, dady. She told me.

Dady...pleese don't cry.

Complications

June 17

Dear diary,

O.K. So here we go. I've finally convinced my husband to start trying for a baby! Took him long enough to say yes, seeing as most of my girlfriends already have 1 or 2 of their own. We're in our 30's for god's sake! But anyway. I'm totes excited! Is 'totes' still a thing? Hmm. (Note to self: Research kids' slang for future reference.)

So we started trying last night. And it was...fun. As usual. We lit some candles. Played an "adult" board game. I swear if it had a "Pass Go" and "Go to Jail" tile, would've been a horny version of Monopoly. So that was... interesting? We made it around the board a couple times before we realized how lost we were. He looked in the box for instructions, but he saw where it said, "Best Played With 3 - 6 Players". 'Swingers Monopoly' is what we've started calling it. It's actually more of a turn off than it is anything else! So, we stuck with our candles. Low, 90's romantic music. We talked. And talked. I've noticed lately how much we do JUST talk! That's why I'm soooooooo glad he agreed to trying! To give us a little extra SPARK in our lives.

Max promised to take a few days vacation after the baby's born to 'nurse us back to health.' He's such a wonderful man. But somewhere, along our relationship, we both lost that passion that we had. This should help both of us find it again. Either that, or separate us! Ha ha.

You know I don't do this often, so I'll write when I can. As always, Thanks for listening.

Julia

September 2,

Dear diary,

YAAAAASSSSSS!!!! It finally happened! It only took about a quarter of a year, but IT HAPPENED! WE'RE PREGNANT! WE'RE PREGNANT! EEEEEEEEEEEE!!!

Don't worry. I'm doing all of this internally, because Max is already deaf from when we found out. Along with the doctors. And nurses. And possibly any children who were in the doctors' office at the time. I'm sure they'll all be fine. I know I WILL. Wanna know why?

Because I'M PREGNANT! I'M PREGNANT!

I can't exactly tell you when it happened, only a small time table: somewhere within the late July early August area. So technically NOT a full 3 months; but it seemed like foooorrreeevvvveerrrr! OMG! And I know he's happy, because I got ridiculous after my second period! I was always all over him and I know the poor guy was exhausted. He even told me a couple times that he was going to hire somebody to do it for him if I didn't let him rest for a few days. He was kidding, of course, but I got scared one day. He called me from work and said, 'I got a guy comin' over…'. Now, it was probably a combination of my lack of sleep cocktailed with my many, MANY mood swings, along with my need for… "attention", but I got nervous that he was serious. And excited that he was serious. But mostly nervous. Maybe.

But, no. He said, 'I got a guy comin' over to look at the sink.' We had had some clog issues that month. He promised he'd get around to it, but of course! You know men.

So. When the guy knocked on the door, I thought, 'What the hell.' I was gonna try my luck anyway. I had gone like 3 days without it, so I wasn't feeling compromisingly. I put my sexiest bra on and threw over my silk nightgown. The one that hangs just above my cheek line. Max loves that one! Sometimes, when we make love, he doesn't even let me take it off! Anyway, I already had my "SPANK ME" panties on, so…there was that. 'Wink'

I rushed down to the door, pushed my boobs together. Shook my messy bun and scrunched my nose, just in case.

I opened it to welcome this big strong woman-hungry man into my home. And maybe, 'into my home'. But when I saw him, it wasn't what I was expecting. Or hoping. He was this man-boobed, four-eyed, faux-hawked, flamer whose shirt was almost tighter than mine. He was…cute, though. He saw my giddy grin drop and said, "Not what you were expecting, huh? It's alright. I get that a lot." He laughed. I grunted and showed him in.

'So you're who my husband called?'

'Well, yeah. Actually, we already work together, but I'm more of the maintenance fella and he asked me to swing by. He is such a sweetheart!'

'That…he is.'

We talked for several minutes. He was very kind. He even left me some of the professional-type drain cleaner he used, along with some tips on how to avoid clogging.

This entry has gone on waaaay longer than I intended. But that was just a hilarious story, and I haven't been able to tell any of my friends about it because they're a bunch of loud-mouths. Now, I just can't let Max read my Diary.

Anyway, as always, Thanks for Listening,

Julia

November 16,

I guess it just wasn't meant to be. Me being a mom and all. We...had...a miscarriage last week. I don't know how it happened. We were going to all of my appointments. Max even took off work a few times to take me. I don't know HOW it could have happened!!! WHY IN THE HELL WOULD THIS HAPPEN! I DID EVERYTHING THE DOCTORS TOLD ME TO DO! I DID EVERYTHING I WAS SUPPOSED TO TO TAKE CARE OF THE BABY! WHY, GOD?! WHY?!? GODDAMMIT!

I've been like this for 4 days now. I've sat in the bathroom for hours at a time. I've laid in bed. I haven't eaten. Max has tried to make me eat, but I can't bring myself to do it! I'm not eating for 2 anymore. I have no reason to eat anymore. I was going to be such a good mom! I was going to spoil him or her, and blame Daddy when they wouldn't act right. I was going to be SUCH A GOOD mom!! Why would God take that from me? Why would he waive such a wonderful gift in my face, just to snatch it away 2 months in?! What kind of cruel joke are you playing at, you bastard!?

LORD. Forgive me. I'm just so...so so so so so...AAAAAAHHHHHHHH!!!! Forget it. I'll continue this entry in a few days. I need more time.

Julia

November 22,

Happy Thanksgiving! There isn't much to be thankful for, except...wine! 3 empty bottles, Diary! 3 empty bottles! And I'm iisn't drunk, yet. Max is drunk. Haaaaa! Ligt-weight, pansy-ass. I'm just here. Talkin to you. On Thanks-fucking-giving! What I ate today, maks up for what I didn't eat for...8 days? I gained to much weight when I WAS PREGNANT, anyway. Maz isn't tryin to help me through my time of need anymore. He's bad. Bad hubsnd. I'mm not crying anymore too though either, cauz I donnnnt thinkk I know how amymore. I'm misspelling words now. O. .k. 1 more glass and then I am done. PRomise! About th o nly good thing about not bing preggo is I can have whatever I fucking want to dringk and as fucking much as i want as well. So, Happpy Thankskgiviiing!

Juuulllluuiiiiiiiiiiiiiiiaaaaaaaaaa

November 23,

Dear diary,

Still...have...a hellacious hangover. Max...OUCH...lemme turn the brightness down on the computer screen real quick...

Max seems to be in a super mood, because when I woke up at...What time is it now? An hour and a half ago, he was eating breakfast next to a cold plate of food that he made for me. I sat down with him, but the smell was GREAT! The feeling it made turning my stomach...Not so much. I pushed it away. I tried to apologize but I couldn't really speak. I put my head in my arm on the table. Wow! Really, Thanksgiving Me? '3 EMPTY BOTTLES'?! Ohhhhh. I never want wine, ever. EVER. again! Or Turkey. Or thanksgiving!

Blah!!!!!!!!!

I think I'm going to go back to bed. Max can take care of the house.

Yeah.

Yeah. Definitely.

Good Night,

Julia

February 6,

Wow! I haven't written anything in a good while now. Feel like I need to start over from the beginning.

Hi, Diary. I'm Julia. It's been 2 and a half months since my last confession. Ha ha. It's been a rough few months. Max's factory shut down in December, so he only got paid furlough for several weeks. Which meant a small Christmas for the families. And we felt so so so bad because everybody got US something, and all we could do was give them a card. PER FAMILY! They all understood, of course, because they're all WONDERFUL! I just hate it so much!

January was...worse.

Max got laid off!! Some B.S. about tax cuts or something! He's only been there 8 months, so sure he was expendable, in SOME cases, I guess. Maybe it's because he was late to work taking me to our pregnancy appointments. And he did take off a few times. But they should have said that! And we had the excuses! I just don't understand some people! This has been THE WORST 4 months of my life! Max has been on unemployment for 2 weeks now. He's looking for more jobs. But it seems like NOBODY in his field is hiring!!! What good does his degree do him if he can't use it?!

I started looking for work too. Retail stores are just coming off from seasonal hires, so pickin's are slim. Restaurants are a no-go for me, because I'm a total germaphobe! Yuck! I guess I'll just have to learn to settle. I have to help out, somehow. After all Max and I have been through, I don't know how much it has really weighed on him. He says he's fine, but he hasn't slept since the lay-off. I just wish I could help. Maybe I'll do something special for him for valentine's day. I know we said we were too old for that kind of stuff, but he deserves it. He really IS a wonderful man! And I thank God everyday for him. Or try to, at least.

Things are going to get better. I know they will.

As always, Thanks for Listening,

Julia

March 25,

Dear diary,

I don't know what to say. How to act. I'm so so so happy! And I'm so so so sooooo scared! I'm pregnant again! Max doesn't know yet. I don't want to tell him. It's nothing like that though! Haha. It's DEFINITELY his! I think I'm done with the desperate housewife thing for good! Either way, though: we're pregnant!!!1!!!!!

I don't know. I started out feeling sick a couple weeks back. And I started getting so lazy but soooooo hungry! I couldn't eat enough! Max joked about our being on a fixed income, and that I needed to slow down. Trust me, Max! I wanted to!!!

I started gaining weight. He didn't notice. Or said he didn't. But when I'd mention it, he'd look away and smile while aggressively shaking my tummy. You know how guys are. They tell you you don't look fat and then BAM! 2 months later you have a double chin and you're up a cup and a half. But still, they "haven't noticed." Aaaaahhhhhhh!!!! I'm hungry again. I just ate 30 minutes ago! And it was BREAD! JUST bread! At least 6 pieces of it! AND IT WAS THE TEXAS TOAST KIND!!!!

Anyway, good news all around: Max got a job at a school. Custodian, but it's something. The last one died in a car crash so they needed one ASAP. Hate it for the other guy, but hey: blessings in disguise, right? He's been on at the school for just about a week, and he seems to...enjoy it? Maybe. Not too fond of the jumpsuit, myself, but the school furnished everything from his coveralls to his cleaning supplies. He noticed it was all old and worn, so he talked to the superintendent about renewing some of the materials. They agreed, if not somewhat begrudgingly. But, only after he broke the rotten mop handle over his knee at a council meeting. I told him that that was a stupid thing to do! Seeing as he'd only been there 2 days! He assured me, 'It needed to be done, Hon!'

I took a home pregnancy test. Twice. A few days between each other, just to be sure. I think I'll tell Max after school Friday. That way we can at least set up an appointment for next week. I won't make him come to any of them, so he doesn't miss work. I'll be alright.

As always, Thanks for Listening,

Julia

April 2,

Dear diary,

It's official! We are approximately 7 and a half weeks pregnant! We just got back from the doctor, and she says there is a strong, rhythmic heartbeat, and that the baby must be extremely "healthy" already based on how big I've gotten! I know. Any other time I would have taken offense, but I'm too ecstatic to care, right now. It'll hit me later, I'm sure.

Now, I told the doctor about our loss last year and asked if there were any EXTRA precautions we could take to avoid another one. It was hard to talk about. But she said, my being...the age I am, could have been a factor. Thinking back on everything we discussed, that blank was pretty much as blunt as I've ever had in a doctor. But, again. DON'T CARE! Right now anyway. So, she told me to go to any store with a pharmaceutical section and pick up some prenatal vitamins. This would insure that we (the baby and I) would be on the right track, and the same page, developmentally. I haven't seen Max so happy in a looong time, either! Like, he wasn't even this way with the first baby! Which is probably why he didn't react as deeply as I did when... we lost it. He's back at work, now. I told him he didn't have to take me to my appointment, but he said, 'I just want to be there when the doctor says this is real! I remember how excited you were the first time. It'll be good to see you brighten up that way again!'

He never smiled so hard as when she confirmed it. I think, now that I think about what he said, the only reason he is so happy is because I am. He's such a wonderful husband! I know I always say that, but he has never once tried my patience in serious situations like this. I know he really cares.

I'm going to take this first dose of vitamins and then I'm going to clean the house!! YAAAYYYY!! I've never had this much energy, EVER!

Thanks for listening,

I'll keep you up to date on the baby's progress!!

Julia

May 1,

IT'S A BOY!!! Oh my goooooshshshshshsh!!!!! I'm sooo happy, but sooooo mad at the same time! Max and I had a bet going, that if it was a boy, he would get to name it. And I would name it if it was a girl! I was going to name HER Maxine Adele. But, you know. Didn't happen. Hmph!

He hasn't decided on a name yet, but I'm sure it's gonna be something like Ozzy Van Halen or whatever. Haha. Neh. I trust him to pick out a half-way, not easily made fun of, name for the baby. Just wish he'd let on what he might have in mind.

So, something weird happened with the gender reveal ultrasound. We could easily see the "Boy" but it was... darker...in the womb? than a normal ultrasound. Just around the edges of the screen though. The nurse wasn't sure if it was the actual ultrasound itself or if it was the machine not picking up properly. She chalked it up to the latter, and claimed it was old equipment. She didn't look too much further into it. But she did up my vitamin intake to 3 pills per dose. Just in case. I've still been eating like a mad-woman, but not gaining as much weight. Guess I can be grateful for that. I'd started losing my girlish figure for a while. Ha ha! Boobs are still filling out though. Max is loooooving that!!! I get twice as much attention as I used to. He still wants sex, of course. Actually. So do I! It's so much better now, too! I'm a lot more sensitive...down there. And it's so much easier to satisfy me. He likes that too. Ha ha.

But I'm going to go eat something. Haven't eaten in about 15 minutes, so I am staaaarvviiiinggggg!

I'll keep you updated!

Julia

May 17,

Dear...diary,

Pregnancy is...alright. I'm still eating like a cow, but I'm starting to lose weight more and more. My belly's getting bigger! Baby's growing! That's for sure! But, unlike when I was gaining, Max has notice my getting thinner. He forces food in me, even when I tell him I'm full. It isn't often that I say no to seconds or thirds. He took me to the doctor today. They did an emergency ultrasound (sound only) to make sure the baby was alright. His heartbeat hasn't slown down at all. But the doctor prescribed me a steroid-type medicine to help me put back on a healthy weight. For my AND the baby's sake. It's like a protein shake. It's definitely protein. And it definitely makes me shake! I took my first dose 3 hours ago. I have to take another one in an hour. I'm dreading it, so bad! It IS a 3 times daily, thing. So I better get used to it. I'm feeling dizzy. I'm going to lay down for a while.

Julia

July 2,

I know it probably seems like I laid down for a GOOD while. Ha ha. I've been so busy preparing the house for the Baby. I haven't had time to sit and write. The steroid has helped me gain weight. Not as much as the doctor would have liked, but more than I do. Now I look like an old woman. My eyes are sunk in, my hair is so thin and stringy. My body...is saggy. Only thing looking good now, is this baby belly. I'm rocking the hell out of it!

And apparently, the doctors haven't fixed their equipment since the gender reveal ultrasound. Only it's gotten worse. All we could make out on the screen was the baby's big head! Ha ha. I made fun of Max saying that he was where the big head came from. He laughed and reminded me that my brother's big head is bigger than his. He does have a big head.

We already have a baby shower date planned. It's going to be on October 12. That's approximately 1 month exactly from the baby's birthdate. I'm so...so...so…

excited...

I'm sleepy again. I've been awake for 45 minutes already. I think it's way past my nap time.

Julia

August 25,

Diary. I'm so scared right now. I have to go into surgery this afternoon for...I DON'T EVEN KNOW WHAT IT IS! Turns out, their monitors weren't broken or outdated at all. Apparently, there's a GERM forming inside of my womb and they have to excise the whole embryonic sac, baby and all to save him!!! WHY DOES THIS KIND OF STUFF HAPPEN!!!?????? I mean, nothing to this extent has ever happened beyond my miscarriage, but why can't I have a normal, healthy pregnancy!!???

Doctors say the baby is fine so far, but they have to perform an emergency cesarean. They say he's going to be kept in an incubator. That the chance of survival, even for a premie of his age, is high. I pray they're right. I knew when I started...smelling...2 weeks ago that I should have gotten checked out then. Would it still have been too late? God, I hope I'm not too late. Anesthesia should wear off a few hours after surgery. I'll keep my computer close so I can keep you updated later. I'm prepped. I'm ready.

Maybe they'll get me looking like a human being after they get the baby situated.

I know that's selfish. I'm actually so scared. For BOTH of us.

They're calling for me now. Wish me luck!

Julia Marie

Born: February 27, 1984
Died: August 25, 2017

Beloved Wife, Daughter, & Mother

Survived by her mother, Susan Deloris; her father, Mark Thomas;
her brother, Mark Conner; her husband, Max Bruce; and her son, Jules Thomas.

As we remember her by reading Psalm 23:

The doctors say that her insides were infested, eaten up by this "germ". They couldn't explain it. They asked about our miscarriage. They asked if we came to the hospital to get "cleaned up". All they could tell me was, "The infection from the miscarriage must have somehow been overlooked during 'clean-up'." That the previous egg must have been left in her stomach and sat festering as a pustule for weeks before growing. When we got pregnant again, the doctor said, the fetus...our son...had begun to meld into the rotten egg. Causing regular complications, but helping him grow steadily inside her I don't understand it. They didn't understand it. They fed me so much B.S. I couldn't remember most of it if you paid me. But here I am. Hovering over this incubator with our. Son? I don't know WHAT that thing is! It's "a baby." Only, it's got a swollen belly and... growths on its head. That "germ"...looks like a mold...has ravaged and stained his body. I don't even know if I want to keep it. Then again, it's what Julia wanted for so long. And that's why I named it...HIM...Jules. In her memory. If this...THING survives, I'll make his mother proud. I'll raise him like a good father should. But I really hope...for EVERYONE'S sake.

He doesn't.

Max.

Tomato Vines

Tomato Vines

Outside of the city limits, between the backwoods and the boondocks, you can always find a house. That old house that needs alittle work and fixing up: with the broken windows and chipping paint; termite eaten wooden planks and missing shingles. Yeah. That house that has seemed abandoned for decades upon decades, never seeing any visitors or occupants. Still, the shrubbery and vegetation has always been well-maintained and full of life.

How? you think, How could such lovely plantation flourish around such a dilapidated old building? Maybe, a descendant of the previous owners, not finding any use in trying to sell the inherited homestead, promised he would keep up the family garden...

You shake that thought off when logically the shack, itself should have been leveled a long time ago; making more room for the vegetable field. Then expanding, of course. You've lived in the town for years. Everyday, passing that abandoned landmark to go to school. And eventually, riding into work. Your love for the countryside caused you to abandon your previous dreams of escaping to the real world, and left you rooted to your old hometown. And, that young-at-heart feeling of adventure beckons you to wander onto that broken-down, rotten-planked, death-trap of a house's lawn, just to sneak a peek...maybe even a taste, of what your friends used to call, "the forbidden fruitation."

After so many years of acknowledging the existence of the ramshackled wood and glass hut, it's a wonder you never even attempted to climb onto the green briar steep leading onto the oddly green yard several feet all around the perimeter. But that wouldn't be the case today. No. Today, you're going to investigate what has caused the greenery to stay so lively. So...lovely. So.

Forbidden.

You don't have anywhere to be today, anyway, right? So you turn off your car and get out. Just as you have second thoughts, that nice summer wind wisps into your nostrils as a calming aroma. It fills your lungs as an external breath of confidence; once you exhale, you are focused on one thing. Those leaves. So lush and inviting. So seemingly happy to see you. The way they dance in the drafts; not shriveling on such a warm day, but embracing it. Almost...waving...signaling you over. Hypnotizing, really.

Ignoring such an allure to the senses would surely be a sin unto nature. Yes. You have to go, now. So you climb onto the mound, dead grass and vines surround the twisted and rusting mailbox. You wonder about the difference in the sprouts just ahead.

Probably just a different kind of sodding, you guess. But just the sight of the spriggins of bold hunter green allows you to leave these curiosities behind as you progress toward the house.

Each step on the soft-compressing blades of grass releases a newfound sense of relaxation; almost as a draining of energy, but not as lethargic. You see the front half of the house is vibrantly lit with the sun's colorful reflection of lillies, roses, and tulips. Holly bushes line the side you're closest to. As you approach you see the beautiful ivy vines have overtaken the "FOR SALE" sign, which was probably more obviously inviting to the now familiar house...

The closer you get to it, the more visually enticing the house seems.

You walk toward the other side of the shrubs, right past the far corner of the house. The intrigue of vegetation stretches out, still, to a lone tree. Full and gorgeous, with a tire swing tied on by a thick, unaging rope.

How can this be? you begin to question your observations, yet again. Another step on the lawn, and you are put back at ease. You take in a breath of harmonic pheromones, and continue toward the back of the shack. You look back at the side of the tree and notice its graying and withered trunk, opposite the ever swinging tire. Not even a leaf on a single branch; you step closer and see where the lovely green turf turns to dead wiry grass. You get a chill. But it isnt from the calm-inducing wind this time. It's from your gut. There is something very wrong about this place. You knew it all along! All your childhood; all your life! You KNEW you shouldn't have come here! You KNEW this wasn't where you were supposed to be! AND YOU KNEW...

you take a step to break from the vicinity...

You knew this was where you were meant to be all along.

You shake your head...You were just thinking something, just now. What was it? You look to the back edge of the house, and see the vegetable garden. That's what it was! wasn't it? You were going to have a look at the luscious, ripe veggies. You first notice the tomato vines...Oddly enough, only a few of them are red and pluckable. The others are still only bulbs, small and green. You decide to leave them here for now, and walk onto the peas on the other side of the back steps. Oh yes. These are very much ready to be taste-tested. Such a loud pop when snapped from their hulls! Oh yes. These peas are ready for harvest. But just as you start pulling and popping the pods from their vines, the wind catches you again. It's pushing you toward the tomatoes again.

But, you say as if someone else is listening, there aren't that many tomatoes...And there are all these peas and other vegetables ready to be picked!

The air is thickened with the scent of the few fresh ripe tomatoes. And you counter your initial thoughts with a quick action to the tomato vines. One is so plump and seducing.

OK, you think; I'll try this ONE. Then I'll let the others grow.

You pull the ripened fruit from its vine and into your teeth. Without contempt, the tomato savorily melts in your mouth, and you drop the small bushel of peas you had in your other hand just so you can get a better grip on this tongue-teasing food. After a few juicy bites, you feel something around your legs; you think the juice may have just dripped onto it, so you pay no attention. After all, the tomato is so delectable. You don't want to interrupt your long-awaited snack. Another bite.

The feeling around you calf gets tighter. Sharper, even. You feel as if your leg is being sliced and mangled downward. You look and see you are wrapped up in the tomato vine! You must have stepped into it while you were ignorantly savoring the fruit. But it keeps getting tighter! You struggle to release; it's like a chinese finger trap: the harder you pull, the more pressure you feel.

You fall to the ground, letting go of the tomato! The vines squeeze you into themselves; you feel pressure as your body is engulfed...Your blood is being drained from your veins! Siphoned into the roots from under the soil. You are dragged down, buried up to your neck. But just before you are thrust completely in, just before you are taken, you look at the half-dead tree. It's sprouting leaves again. It's coming back to life. And you are fading into death.

You knew all along. This wasn't where you were supposed to be. Your entire childhood. Your entire life. You KNEW you never should have come here. YOU KNEW this would be your fate. And Mother Nature...

Thanks you.

Guardians Of The Gods

A young group of students wandered the darkened trails of a local cemetery on Halloween Night, in search of a legendary mausoleum, said to have been built *even* before the town itself existed.

--Typical urban myth claimed that the tomb was developed by a satanic group of nomads, who worshipped there after each sacrificial kidnapping. The victims' bodies were methodically dissected and drained of blood. The skin was removed, and sutured together as ritual garments. The organs were burned as a "meal for the Gods". And what flesh was left, was dined on by the occultists. The bones were stored within the walls of the structure. It is said to have been the home of so many brutal killings, that skeletons packed inside have left the interior so cramped, so crowded, that entry would be nearly impossible without stepping on the remains of a once-living human.--

But tonight, as fate would have it, these eight would open the sealed chamber in search of notoriety beyond comprehension. Well, as far as adolescence goes. But in their journey to discover the realities behind the Veil, they open much more than an ancient burial plot. They open much, much more...

"WHAT THE HELL, MARCUS?!" shouted a young lady, donning a thrown-together witch costume.

Marcus laughed, in an attempt to justify his actions.

"*What the hell, Julian??*" he mocked back at his sister. "Don't tell me you're getting scared, *now!* It was *your* idea to come on this stupid hike with the BOZO Brigade!"

"Shut up, you jerk! They're my friends!" Julian defended the wandering.

A small voice peaked from among the group,

"Yeah! We're her friends!"

Marcus gasped sarcastically, "Oh! I'm sorry, pipsqueak!" He rustled the boy's skeleton bald cap, "I didn't mean to offend you!"

His older sister retaliated again, "Shut up, Marcus."

She put her arm around the child's shoulders, pushing him forward, gently.

"It's ok, Shawn. Catch back up with the others."

Shawn pouted, "But I wanna stay back here with you."

Marcus, again, feigning compassion sighed,

"Awww, Julian! I fink the widdle baby skeleton might have a widdle baby crush."

Julian raised her hand to threaten her younger brother, "SHUT UP, MARCUS! GOD!"

She pushed the youngest of the crowd closer to their huddle, while the others talked among themselves.

"No you don't, sweetie." she looked back at Marcus, and rolled her eyes

"I don't even want to stay back here. Let's get closer to the front."

Marcus chuckled silently, waving his hands at his sister. She punched his arm and walked ahead.

"Yeah," his humor had evaporated, "screw you, too! Two...Screw you two, too!"

The two ignored his last nefarious taunt.

Shawn whispered to his babysitter, "Why did you invite *him*, Julie?"

They squeezed into the group from behind, her arms around the young boy,

"Ugh," she groaned in disgust "I ask myself that *every* time."

She looked back at the mid-teen jock, spiraling a football up and down;

"But this time," she tickled Shawn's shoulders "I did it to scare him silly!"

They both laughed.

Chi-Chi, groaning like a miserable mule, dragged sluggishly beside his "best friend," Landon, the navigator.

"Aw, man. I don't know why I agree to do things with you. It's like, every time I wanna hang out, you're all, '*nuh, man. I'm busy, and stuff.*' But when you call me, I'm like, 'Totally, dude! Let's rock!' And we always end up in some sort of BS situation." He put his hands to the sides of his head and paused, "Like, how the hell did we end up in a graveyard, dude? REALLY?! A FRICKIN' GRAVEYARD, LAN?!"

Landon scoffed at his friend's over dramatization, and rustled the map.

"Well, Chich," he began, **"A**: *You* never wanna do *anything* cool. **B**: I'm *always down* to do something cool. **C**: It's like a scavenger hunt in 'A FRICKIN' GRAVEYARD'!" Landon took Chi-Chi by the sleeve of his pirate costume, "I mean: Who *wouldn't wanna* do it? And most importantly... **D**: We got about 2-½ sets trailin' with us. Hell! Even *you* might get lucky." He elbowed the chubby, latino-descendent with a "CHK-CHK" noise, before walking on.

Chi-Chi stopped in his tracks, "But, there are *four* girls with us."

Landon returned to collect his "first mate" by wrapping his arm around Chi-Chi's head, irritating his ears, while he scrambled audibly in pain.

"Yeah," Landon said, now pulling the fat boy by his ear, "but Julian is just about a C... *maybe* a C+..."

Chi-Chi squirmed away from Landon during his continued rating of their female companions,

"... and Kim..." He took a deep, disappointed breath, **"Kim** is like... kindergarten-flat, man. I mean, I'd be afraid of catching a charge if I messed with her." He groped his buddy one last time, "But how 'bout this: *you* can have her! The worst thing the cops can do to you is... deport ya!" he pushed his victim away as he laughed and trotted ahead.

Chi-Chi halted in his steps again, "I was born here, asshole!"

Zira, the most outspoken of the feminine trio of Kim and Sasha, drew herself in from the chapping wind through the tombstones,

"Sasha? Girl, why are we doin' this, again? I mean, I get that it's Halloween and all, but when I met you, I did *not* sign up for this 'goin' walkin' after midnight-horror movie mess'! I was just ready to stay at Kim's house; put on a Romero flick; curl up with some popcorn and pass out about halfway into the movie. You know: like we do *every year!*"

Having just heard what Landon said about her, Kim began walking slower than her two girlfriends, but still within whisper range; she huffed,

"Yeah, Sash. I'm not really up for this treasure hunt thing, anymore. Can't we just leave?"

Sasha, who always spoke with the confidence she had accumulated as "Miss Popularity", all of her life, put her arms around the girls' waists,

"Well…ladies…" she cleared her throat, "*I'm* here because Little Miss Goody-Two Shoes back there's brother is here. OK? Like, he went from Zero to Adonis within a year and a half. And, I don't know if that magic potion he drank is going to wear off as quickly, so I'm gonna go ahead and try and hit that, just in case. *Peaches and Cream?*" She snarled her nose with a chuckle.

Zira stared at her overly-confident counterpart, mouth agate.

"You're kidding, right?"

Sasha shook her head with the same eager smile.

"He's like, *two* years younger than you!" Zira protested, "You're about to be 18! That *literally* makes him *off limits!*"

Sasha humphed in consideration, "Not yet, **Z**. I still have a week before *I'm* legal. So, I *guess* I'll have to get some of that beforehand, then, huh?"

Kim, drawn into her overshirt from the cold, contested as well.

"You're going to hell."

Sasha flicked her head at the pale, strawberry-blonde.

Kim continued before she noticed Sasha's new, unenthused demeanor, "You are so…so going to…"

Finally realizing, she stifled herself a bit. "You're so wrong."

Sasha giggled, "See ya there, Cowgirl!" She yelped like an excited country hick.

Zira spoke her final piece, "Alright! But when that Julian chick kicks your ass, I am *not* helping you!

The arrogant teen scoffed with a snort,

"Yeah. I think you mean, 'if she *tries*.' I doubt she even knows how to scrap: 'Little Miss Perfect'"

The timid Kim spoke again, in Julian's defense,

"Well, I don't know. Back in middle school, I watched her throw down with one of the P. E. teachers."

She lowered her voice in a gossipy tone, "She said he tried touching her in the locker room."

Hastening her speed, Sasha ignorantly brushed off the girls' warnings,

"Yeah, yeah. Who cares? I'm still gonna bone her brother."

Kim raised her voice a bit,

"Well, I'm just sayin', *she can fight*. And if you're not careful, you're gonna find out first-hand!"

Sasha, speeding up even more, threw her hand behind her as if to block Kim's last remarks,

"Yeah. OK, 'Kindergarten'-Cups."

She walked ahead to Landon.

Zira wrapped her arm around Kim, "'Sokay, Baby Girl." She comforted in a warming tone, "We're almost there."

Kim dropped her head.

Julian, having listened closely as the other girls conspired, put her guard up and whispered,

"You're damn right, 'you'll find out.'"

Shawn perked up, "Find out what?"

Julian rubbed Shawn's shoulders, "Nothing, Sweetie. Nothing."

Sasha, conveying slight interest in Landon, approached the teen,

"So, *Columbus*, how much farther?"

Landon fumbled, unprepared for Sasha to talk to him, much less approach, responded,

"Oh! Uh…um…" he stammered; then breathing out through his tightly compressed lips, sprayed a splash of saliva onto the map.

Sasha reflexed back in disgust

"Crap! I'm sorry!" he began wiping the spit from the map onto his shirt, in a panicked haste.

Chi-Chi more comfortable now than he was a few moments earlier, doubled over in laughter, almost unable to breathe.

"Good. . ." he mustered between breaths, ". . . good job, pal." His vocality returned, "Real smooth!"

Landon whispered forcefully backward, "Shut up, doucher!"

He took a moment to collect himself, then exhaled more calmly,

"Well, it's hard to say. Ya see, this map looks kind of old. And a lot of these tombstones look the same."

Sasha expressed her exasperation with a huff, "So...you have no idea where we are?"{

Landon put the map back down and cut his eyes at Sasha again,

"I mean, YEAH! I know exactly where we are!"

Chi-Chi shouted from behind the two, "Let the man drive, woman!" He laughed under his breath.

Sasha scoffed again.

"Is this even the right cemetery?"

She turned to walk to the back of the group.

Landon looked down at the map, raising his voice behind him,

"Uh. . . yep! Yeah! Definitely the right cemetery! Just a couple more plots and we should…"

He lowered his voice again, "...she's gone, isn't she?"

His faithful sidekick nodded, "She's gone."

The navigator reaffirmed, "Yeah. She's gone."

Chi-Chi patted Landon's bicep then whispered with a sigh, "Strike Two, buddy!"

Landon brushed his hand away,

"Go to hell, Taco-Taint."

The eight drew closer to the crypt.

Julian watched Sasha walk towards the back of the group; as she passed, Julian grabbed her arm, "Where do you think you're going?"

The horned seventeen-year-old began picking Julian's fingers off one-by-one,

"Oh," she shrugged, "nowhere. Just coming to talk to Marcus for a minute."

She continued past.

The jock's older sister clasped her witchy fingers back around Sasha's humorous, now more tightly,

"Like hell, you are!"

Sasha pressed her face into her adversary's personal bubble and gritted,

"Oh yeah, baby. It's gonna be hotter than hell, and sweeter than candy."

She giggled heartlessly,

"Once I get done 'talking' to him, you're going to have lock him up to keep him away from me."

The angsty teen licked Julian's red, furious cheek.

The 'witch' swung her other arm around and pulled Sasha to the ground,

"He's my brother, you skanky, little--"

Marcus grabbed his sister by her shoulders to lift her off from the agitator,

"LET ME GO!" she squabbled, "I'M GONNA KILL 'ER!"

Little Shawn pumped his fist up and down,

"Yeah! Go Julie! Go!"

Zira pulled Julian's charge up to her and Kim.

She rubbed his back as if nudging him forward, "No, baby. No. Don't get in the middle of that."

Julian, still kicking and screaming, was shortly brought to a calm.

Landon shouted from a few more steps ahead of the pack, "Hey, guys! GUYS!"

He turned slightly towards the others,

"I think this is it!"

They beheld the monolithic mausoleum, and stood in awe of the behemoth catacomb.

Julian had stopped struggling. Marcus released her to help Sasha back to her feet; dusting her off. Zira, Kim, and Shawn gathered next to Chi-Chi and Landon.

The structure was capped with a stained-glass steeple. The moon shone directly through one side and cast a reflection out from the other. The casting colored the grown up weeds beside a neighboring plot. The ever-rising satellite could read the time, it seemed, by the stretching reflection of the dyed glass. The group, seemingly abandoning the skirmish, once again, formed a mob and entered the tomb. Inside, the wretched stench of molding matter and dust-wrapped, decaying bone swirled between the eight. The moon had reached a high enough point in the sky, where it shined through the tempered glass.

Alas, there was light! The momentary blackened walls of the sarcophagal hut were now painted by the hues of the lunar beams shining through the top of the steeple. The colors were so magnificent, the group had almost forgotten they were among dozens of dead, once-humans. ALMOST, being the key word. They were all slapped back into reality when the youngest, Shawn, stepped backward onto a femur bone. It rolled from beneath his heel, causing him to slip into a whole other pile of skeletons.

The boy scrambled to get up, resulting in only his kicking around ribs and vertebrae.

"AH! AAAAHHHHHH!" he shrieked in a panic as he tried reaching towards his babysitter,

"**JULIEEE!** HELP ME!!!"

Everyone shuffled around until Shawn was back on his feet. By the time he realized he was alright, so did everybody else. And they shared a solemn laugh after.

The place was softly lit, now.

Landon stood on a concrete slab, stained with what one would imagine was dried blood. This must have been the sacred sacrificial bed used to splay the victims, whether recently dead. . . or otherwise, during the horrendous rituals. As he ascended, the air around him thickened with an overbearing cool; and an even worse aroma. He paid no mind. After all, this was a home for the dead

Speaking louder than usual, but still wary of excess volume, he began, "Welcome, friends! To a new Halloween Tradition. Future generations will look back on this historic night, and wish they were here! As I hold in my hands, instructions! Instructions to commune with the dead! And, toni--"

Marcus broke his silence after remaining "the black sheep" for the past several minutes.

"GET ON WITH IT, LOSER!"

He was the most popular boy in the group. The only one to shatter the school's football record in the past decade. He could've said anything, and with the exception of Julian and Shawn, everyone would have listened. So, naturally, a blunder of impatience followed his interruption.

Sasha didn't miss a beat, "Yeah, Haywood!" She mocked, "What's with the dialogue?! Are we gonna do this, or what?"

Shawn was now tucked safely back into Julian's arms, and spoke with a pouty voice,

"Yeahhhh. . . Come on, I'm tired!"

Julian turned to Sasha and with a laughing choke,

"And it's monologue. . ." then softened her tone as she turned back, "Bitch"

With his friend's neglectful teasing ever-present on his mind, Chi-Chi joined in with the crowd, formed a tunnel with his hands around his mouth,

"Yeah, Shakespeare! It's gonna be Thanksgiving by the time we get to. . . whatever it is we're supposed to be doing!"

The original speaker dropped his hands with the map and "instructions" still clenched within them. Looking down at Chi-Chi with a sense of betrayal. He responded with a low, and stern besmirching,

"Really, **CHICH?** You too?"

Chi-Chi shrugged, "One of us has to look like less of a loser. . . despite its inevitability".

He looked at the three girls, and poking an elbow at Zira, "'Look like less of a loser,' try saying that five times fast!"

The girls just gazed, unamused.

The Latino turned back to his "long-winded" friend with a slight sense of embarrassment, "Just get on with it, Lan!"

Landon jumped to the end of his well-practiced speech in disappointment with everyone's reactions.

Now uninspired, "Ugh! Fine! Does everybody have what I told you to bring?"

Kim turned her backpack to the front, as Sasha and Zira began digging through it. Julian pulled a shot glass from her jacket. The other three girls each grabbed a candle from inside the bag. Marcus held a lighter. And Chi-Chi lifted a pencil and notepad in the air, smiling as a dog might when scratched behind the ears. Little Shawn searched his pockets for something to show: but to no avail.

The boy whined in a bit of panic,

"I didn't know I was s'posta bring nothin'!"

Marcus crouched down behind Shawn, and said in a low, malicious, tone,

"But you did, kid." He grabbed the juvenile, "YOU'RE THE SACRIFICE!"

Marcus, Sasha, Zira, and Chi-Chi laughed a little when Shawn let out a tiny yelp.

He shut his eyes, and squoze himself back into Julian,

"No no no no no no no no! Don't let them sacrifice me, Julian! Please!"

The babysitter turned the boy to face her. Shawn opened his eyes, fear still welled into the pits.

Julian comforted him, "Listen, Shawn; you know that's not true. I brought you because your parents needed me to keep you while they went out."

She tapered into a more humorous tone, "And they pay me to make sure you remain in *one piece*, so. . . there ya go."

Shawn smiled a little, with his heart slightly more at ease

The two giggled to each other.

Landon, still gripping the map in the air, chimed in sarcastically,

"Awe. Hallmark moment."

Silence fell among the group for just a moment.

The boy on the slab continued, "Aaand back to me!"

He tried pumping the crowd up one last time,

"Tonight, we are going to open a portal! Allowing ourselves to see what awaits us. . ." he pulled a stick of chalk from his pocket with his free hand, ". . . behind the Veil of this so-called 'Reality'!"

Sasha gasped in awe,

"Ooo! Is that a crystal?"

Everyone turned to stare at the Deviless, followed by a couple putting their heads down, to stifle a laugh.

Looked down at the, obviously, confused cheerleader-type, then back at the chalk and scoffed,

"What? What-no. . ."

He let down his hand to show her,

"No. It's chalk, honey. . ." He sighed, "What. . .?"

Julian glances at Sasha to whisper,

"That is literally the stupidest thing you've EVER said, since I've known you."

Sasha reciprocated the snarl, and shrugged, murmuring to herself more than anyone else,

"Honest mistake."

Landon hopped down from the concrete altar, huffing,

"OK! We only have a few hours to get this done, so. . . without *further* delay. . ."

He pointed to Marcus without even looking, ". . . wanna shut the door?"

Marcus obliged.

Landon proceeded to scribble on the slab. And almost instantaneously, the others cast in their contributions. Marcus lit the girls' candles. Zira, Sasha, and Kim, placed them on both sides and above the existing chalk marks. Julian set the shot glass next to Landon's scrawling hand. Chi-Chi leaned on the other side of the table to begin "documenting" the night's events. They all gathered as closely to the altar as they could; circumventing it, as if they wanted to see what was being written; still, keeping their distances at the same time. Nobody knew what to expect. Even though the scribe coordinated the entire gathering, he didn't believe what he held to be real. Once surrounding, the others could see what he had designed: it was a makeshift spirit board. And a halfway decent one at that; considering the time he took to make it. Everything was in the right place and order: "YES" and "NO" in the upper corners. The alphabet, arched and paralleled with thirteen letters on both sets. Numbers 1-0 beneath them. And finally, "GOODBYE" delineating the bottom edge. He even drew the moon and sun at the apex of the "board" for flair.

Zira was most uncomfortable with the etchings as her family was very religious, and she understood the gravity of the OUIJA.

She began backing away, shaking her head, obviously nervous,

"No. Hell nah. I'm not doin' this." She contested.

Sasha looked at her terrified friend, laughing lightly,

"Come on, Z! It's just a little Halloween fun!"

Zira looked at Kim.

Kim, still huddled into herself, looked back at Zira. She shook her head, as well: unsure, but willing to continue,

"Yeah. It's just a stupid game. Let's just play and then we can go home. We can eat the leftover candy from my little brother's trick or treating spree." She laughed softly but nervously.

Landon took the rattled seventeen-year-old by the wrist, firm but gently.

"You can't leave, now. We've already begun." His demeanor had shifted. It was clear that he had become more serious about this "game". "The door. . . is sealed."

Zira peered, almost sickly, at the leader of the group; but ultimately, resiliently, conceded to staying.

Landon turned back toward the center, and spoke more softly,

"Now, as we continue: let us hold hands. And close our eyes. Let our spirits and energies fuse into one. Let ourselves become the power of which we seek."

He continued holding Zira's hand, and lay his other on the table for Kim to take. She took Chi-Chi's wrist. Zira grabbed Shawn's fingers. While, of course, Shawn remained with Julian; she then clasped onto Marcus. Marcus met back to Sasha. All gripped each other gently, at first. Then tighter. And within a moment, the dimly lit chamber glew like a light had been switched on. It wasn't the subtle hues cast by the moon. It wasn't the intensely burning candles. The aura of the temple, seemed to gather with cool blue pigment. But the air within was warm. Comfortably warm. The group's "energies" had developed as a mass of light, showing over the eight. This was described in the instructions, which Landon had studied rigorously since the "map" came to him.

Now, it was time to begin.

Landon released his grip from Zira and Kim, before looking around the room.

He sternly commanded, "You can let go of each other, now. But, stay focused."

Everyone opened their eyes with disbelief as they acknowledged the difference inside the temple. They each dropped the other's hands, with the exceptions of Shawn and Julian, and Sasha and Marcus. Sasha gave Julian a cold glare. But the jock's sister pretended to ignore the nefarious gesture.

Landon turned the transparent shot glass upside-down and placed it over each letter to ensure they were spaced out well enough. He recentered it, and leaned inward,

"Now, if everyone can touch the glass."

The eight did so.

"Lightly!" he directed, "One or two fingers, should suffice; then repeat after me:

'SPIRITS WITHIN THIS HOLY PLACE. . .

Everyone repeated, as ordered. They continued,

"'IF YOU ARE STILL HERE, SHOW US SOME TRACE. . .

'WE CALL TO YOU FROM THE REALM OF BREATH. . .

'WE WISH TO SEE INTO YOUR LAND OF DEATH. . .

'WE PRAY ADMISSION TO PEEK BEHIND. . .

'THE CURTAINS OF LIFE, WHICH KEEP US BLIND. . .

'READY OR NOT; WE'RE ALMOST IN. . .

INHALE, DEEP. . . LET'S BEGIN!"

Landon elaborated on the the typical rules for summoning spirits. . . as well as some atypical ones:

"OK, guys. Rules are simple: We ask questions to get answers. Don't take your fingers off the cup. . . Only one allowed to is CHICH. He's recording everything. And If things get too creepy, all we have to do is move to the word 'GOODBYE,' and it'll all be over."

Julian huffed impatiently, "OK. Yeah, yeah. I'm pretty sure we've all seen the movies. . . YouTube videos. . . we know the rules."

Marcus still cradling the football in arm, spoke with a slight pause,

"Wait. . . so, why can't we take our fingers off the shot glass?"

Landon scoffed, "DUH! Because. . . ya know. . . your soul would get trapped. . ."

His explanation rose to an eerie yet sarcastic tone,

"Trapped. . . in the Realm of the Dead! OoOoOo!"

Julian said under her breath,

"You're so full of it. . ."

The original speaker cut in, "We're inside of a two-century old human slaughterhouse. The instructions are very strictly set. Very finely. If they aren't followed, to a T. . ."

He tightened his throat into an ominous growl, ". . . who knows what could happen."

The 'witch' replied in sarcasm,

"Oh, har har. Real nice, loser. Can we just. . ."

She signaled frustratedly back toward the "spirit board."

Landon chuckled,

"Of course. *Absolutely!* Unless anybody else wants to waste moonlight. . ."

A second pause hung over them . . . silence. . .

"Excellent!" he cried more enthusiastically, "Now, who wants to ask the first question?"

Naturally, Nobody wanted to "ask a drinking dish a question," from fear of looking stupid. So, it being Landon's experiment, took it upon himself.

"OK. Nobody else wants to start: I guess I'll be the first:"

He sighed,

"Is there anybody in here with us?"

After a few moments with no response, he tried again:

"Are there any spirits who want to communicate with us?"

Marcus joked,

"Speak now, or forever hold your peace!"

Again, there was no reply. Not even a shudder. The air remained warm. Light and thick. But still, there was an uneasiness among the friends. So much, in fact, Zira had to acknowledge it.

She removed her hand from the glass, like a reflex. Then looked at Landon,

"Landon, man; this is stupid. Can we go?!"

Upon her detaching from the dish, there was a rattle which stirred among the group, but was only noticed by a couple. Then, the makeshift planchette glided over to the word "NO", as the group looked at the fearful young lady. The others' eyes now roamed around the table; sharing skeptical stares.

Zira also noticing the ever so slight movement on the "board," attempted to remain unfazed.

She grunted irritatedly, "You're *so* funny, guys!"

She turned to leave, "Screw this!"

As she made her way to the entrance, from which they came, but found it as Landon had stated earlier, "sealed."

"Come on, guys!" She threw her hands up, "This really isn't fun anymore!" She lowered her voice to appeal more calmly to the few, "Marcus, baby, open the door."

But, something else happened. She saw the others direct their attention back to the board. There were laughs among the remaining seven, and claims of "I didn't do it" rang throughout. They no longer paid the outcast any mind.

Poor Zira raised her voice again, more angrily, now,

"HELLO!!???"

Nobody listened.

Still sort of laughing, the ringleader asked again,

"OK, OK! Who's next?"

Marcus sniffled humorously,

"I got one! I got one!"

He composed himself and cleared his throat,

"Will my team win out this year?"

Everyone else groaned at the silly question.

Chi-Chi looked at Marcus with a nearly disgusted disposition,

"Really, dude? You're gonna waste the ghosts' time with a question like that?! Why don't you just ask it what color underwear you're wearing!"

The glass began moving, again; the group read the letters aloud as Chi-Chi wrote them down, still trying to keep one finger on the planchette.

Their voices rumbled as a collective,

"C...O...M...M...A...N...D...O...

Marcus snatched his hand away, trying to look more furious than embarrassed. Sasha looked at him, then at his shorts, then back at his face, biting her bottom lip with an enamored smirk. The others just giggled, repeatedly.

The jock then noticed someone out of the corner of his eye. Someone was standing at the door.

It's Zira! He thought.

"Z? What the hell are ya doin'?" he walked towards her, "Why are you over here? Why are you by yourself?"

Zira looked at the boy approaching. She lashed out, on the verge of tears, "Oh! Now you notice me, huh! Y'all are over there playin' that stupid game. And all I wanna do is leave. I've been here the past five minutes! Why ya worried about me, now?!"

A disconcerted look of bewilderment gleamed across his face.

He asked, half smiling, "Five minutes?"

He chuckles, "I just saw you ten seconds ago, over there."

The girl leaned off from the door,

"Are you high, or somethin'??"

In the background, the friends continued their "game". Periodically asking random questions, but mostly never getting any response.

Marcus put his hands up in surrender,

"OK. Sorry! My mistake. I'm comin' back to the game."

He began to turn away, "Feel free to jump in, yourself."

He walked to where he once stood at the altar, but somebody else was already standing between his sister and Sasha. He looked across the way to find Zira back in the circle; all the while the others were enjoying themselves a bit too much.

Still, out of the corner of his eye, he saw a figure at the door again. He knew what he THOUGHT *wasn't* possible. He walked around to where Zira stood and gazed at the man who took his place. The jersey and eyes were familiar. As were the hair and dull smirk. Marcus stared at. . . himself. . . for what he interpreted as several minutes. And just in awe of the unlikelihood of it. Then he saw Zira. . . in front of him. And he saw her. . . at the entrance. And he saw himself. . . looking. . . at himself. . . looking. . . at. . . everybody else. . .The two remained silent. To themselves, as though mourning the loss of a loved one; and preferring to segregate from everybody else.

The group played on.

"WHAT THE HELL?" Marcus fought the pseudo-realization, "Was LANDON right? Are we ON the Other Side?!"

Chi-Chi raised his voice in excitement, with a tender chuckle beneath it,

"Who will I marry?"

As a young adult, the heavy fellow immediately regretted asking this question aloud. Especially, since the others' overtones had dissipated just prior. Subtle laughter rattled through the bones, which were seemingly forgotten shortly after the eight had entered. Marcus' corporeal existence moved, slightly, with the pushing of the shot glass. And he seemed to communicate, physically and often verbally with the rest of the pack. Once his ethereal self witnessed this, his will had shattered.

Who was controlling his body?

How was it even possible?

A breathy, light female voice replied to his mental questions,

"Anything. . . is possible. . ."

Then faded out. Even for such a small declaration, the words seemed strained. Excruciatingly efforted.

Having noticed the slack-jawed visage of her current fling, Sasha decided to up the "game" for a little more excitement. She suddenly realized that nobody had asked the "spirit's" name. And corrected the foul, directly by cocking her attitude, ever-so slightly,

"I've got a question"

A pause grabbed the group.

"Who are we talking to?"

Landon, not succumbing to the fact that his chances with the girl had long since flown, rooted her on,

"Oooo! That's a good one, Sash!"

Silence, once more, within the tomb. It was almost like, *this* was the question it had been waiting for. Or maybe, it was just that time of night. Perhaps the calling of the moon. The placement of its rays. The lifting of the Veil. The Entrance. . . of an Entity. Or were there. . . many?

After a few mere seconds, the candles went out.

The cheerleader looked at Chi-Chi,

"Jeez, Tubs! Breathe much?!"

The fat sidekick shrugged in confused offense,

"It wasn't me!"

Suddenly, the map rose into the center of the table and began to singe, with no flame whatsoever. Shawn took his hand from the makeshift planchette to cover his eyes, turning quickly to safety in Julian's stomach. He whimpered. The burnings danced around the paper, like fairies in a meadow. They started shaping into a hideously deformed face. And though, on the paper, created dimension so perfect. . . so viscerally wrenching, the remaining five shook.

Julian, for the sakes of Shawn and herself, had to stand against whatever this was. She betrayed only a few with her facade of skepticism,

"Landon, you're so full of it!"

Genuinely apprehensive, the naive leader retaliated,

"What the hell, Jules?! What do ya mean!?? I'm not doing this!"

The babysitter relentlessly phished for a confession,

"Oh, *whatever*, you prick! Cut it out!"

She tucked the child in closer,

"Can't you see this little boy's scared to death!"

Again, Landon rebuttaled, "And can't *you* see: I'm not smart enough to rig something like this up!!"

The paper smoldered for moments among the feuding teens. As Kim and Chi-Chi looked on, their paralytic entrancement heightened, then. . . Kim. . . broke free:

She shouted, uncharacteristically,

"SAY GOODBYE! SAY GOODBYE!"

It was a good idea.

But as they started to slide the glass onto the chalked farewell, the powder smeared away by what could only be considered as a phantom brush. There was no longer a GOODBYE to bid. There were only Landon, Sasha, Chi-Chi, Kim, and Julian. And they were trapped. . . by whomever they were talking to, just ten minutes earlier.

Marcus stood off from the wall as he saw what had begun to transpire. He ran back to Zira,

"SOMETHING'S HAPPENING!"

He shook the girl, pulling her vertical,

"GET UP! SOMETHING'S HAPPENING!"

She crumbled back to the ground, too groggy and lethargic to care about ANYTHING that seemed to be going on, "No, it's not, Marcus."

She waved the boy off,

"No, it's not. Just go play your game. I'll be right here when the rest of you are ready to leave!"

He dropped Zira's arm, after turning to see exactly *what* was happening,

"What. . . the. . ."

Now, what Marcus saw was nothing one would be familiar with. It could never be explained as one would describe a landscape to an artist, but rather the elaboration of an impressionists painting to the blind.

Within the circle, he noticed the bending of the blue aura in the middle of the room. It was translucent; with the consistency of gelatin. He stumbled around to observe portraits of sorts, peering out from the catacomb walls. And they multiplied, the more he looked. Some of these transformed, and became whole as full-bodied apparitions. The map wasn't floating, from what he could see: he approached it as closely as possible. The "gelatinous" figure held it to its face; and its image burned through. Unsure as he was, Marcus stood among the unseen. And listened as they spoke.

Another female voice came through; not so labored as the first, but still breathing heavily between each few words,

"They aren't. . ." a breathy wind swept, "They're the. . ."

The creature's speech just didn't hold up for mortal ears to hear. But the words, when comprehended, were oh-so unsettling:

"We haven't had this many. . ." Another heavy breath, "That fat one looks yummy!"

Marcus watched the figure slide effortlessly across the room, touching the back of Kim's neck and then taking hold of Chi-Chi's shoulders. For a moment, the pale, cautious, girl was frozen. Then, she broke free. The paralyzed Latino, however, stayed shackled by the spirit's embrace. She licked his bulgy chin, so sadistically, it was close to sexual satisfaction; and the once vibrant color began to drain from his face.

The first unknown voice fluidly became a distant laugh; repeating higher to lower, and over and over.

Julian, still disregarding the reality of all that was happening, asked again, while Sasha huddled herself against the nearest wall, "WHO ARE YOU???"

And again, there came a quiet. . . from her standpoint, at least. This was followed by a guttural retching of several vibrations from Landon's direction. So, this only "proved" his participation in the prank. She attempted to call him out on it, but was halted by the otherworldly bellowing as it audibly climbed from the boy's abdomen into his chest. . . through his esophagus. . . and finally, from his unnaturally widening mouth.

The thunderous voice was more masculine. . . more feral, than Landon could have falsified, as it roared, "I. AM. GOD!!!"

Landon uncontrollably lifted the shot glass and smashed it, whereas only a jagged shard remained on the perfectly round bottom. He lifted his shirt, beginning to carve symbols and letters into his torso. He bled while he laughed. As *he* cried. His hand levitated towards his face and sporadically plunged the broken glass into each eye. The boy was helpless to whatever this was abusing him. But it quickly ended once he lowered the crystal blade, sliding it deep into his throat; severing his jugular and carotid artery.

His body fell.

During this gruesome display, Julian, Kim, and Sasha completely lost their minds. Marcus and Zira's unhosted bodies reacted. . . numbly. . . for lack of a better description; unfazed by the tragedy laid in front of them.

Chi-Chi remained comatose as the spectre sucked the life force from his nostrils.

Young Shawn, trying to block out all he had heard, recognized a voice calling to him.

It was his mother's voice, beckoning to him from the corner of the Mausoleum,

"SHAWN? Shawn, Sweetheart. . . Are you alright?"

The boy cried back,

"MOM?!"

The voice, so soft and endearing, spoke again,

"Yes, baby! Mommy's here!"

Not hearing what the kid had, Julian began to inquire angrily as to why he had, all of a sudden, begun to tug himself away from her.

Panicked, she called back to him, "SHAWN? Shawn, Sweetie! Where're you going?! SHAWN!!"

The child ignored his babysitter to follow the sound of "his mother's" sweet, songlike voice, whimpering,

"MOM!? WHERE ARE YOU!!!????"

The unseen vox grew lower, softer, but more sinister,

"I'm right here, baby. . ."

Shawn drew in closer to the almost pitch black corner. The air around him grew still. His existence had traversed into *That* Realm, where he met. . .

The Voice;

It was much softer now,

"I'm. . ." it faded, slightly, "here. . ."

And then, again. . . a final momentary silence.

The once-unseen spectre screamed with the most mountainous of horrors,

"COME TO MAMA!!!!!"

Shawn fell to his butt, crying harder and louder than before

Shawn squealed in a high-pitched squall,

JULIE!!!

The babysitter raced over to the corner to pick up her charge, still ignorant to why he walked away to begin with. She saw he was just as frightened as everyone else, and pulled him to the door.

She knelt down in front of him, teary-eyed but trying to be fearless for the boy,

"Shawn. Shawn, Sweetie; I need you to get out of here, OK? Can you do that for me?! Can you do that, Sweetie?

Shawn nodded, panickedly.

"OK." Julian continued, "OK. Just get out of here and run to the nearest adult, and you bring them here! OK?"

She turned the child around and pulled the handle.

It wouldn't budge.

She pulled harder. Still, nothing. She pulled and pulled and pulled, until. . . the handle broke off. . .

"SHIT!!!"

She threw the cast iron door piece to the ground.

Sasha was out of her wits with fear. She lay on the ground, trembling and shaking her head in denial, praying she would wake up. Kim tried swaying Zira away from the altar, but her body was stuck. Half-in-Half-out. She wouldn't snap out of it. Completely stirring from anxiety, Kim shook herself out of a constant breakdown. She then attempted to get Marcus's attention.

Kim nervously tugged Marcus's jersey,

"MARCUS! MARCUS!"

After she received no response, she yanked more violently,

"WHAT THE HELL IS WRONG WITH YOU?! WE NEED TO GET OUT OF HERE! MARCUS!"

Having had enough, she impulsively slapped him,

"Oh! I am so, so sorry!"

The shock caused the jock to slingshot back into his senses. He didn't see Zira at the door anymore. Besides the chaos of the invisible world's wrath in his wake, everything looked. . . normal? He wasted no time to get to the concrete door. He pounded and pounded and kicked and thrust himself into it. To no avail, he tried something else. He began jerking on the iron barred window. It gave. A little at a time. Until it, too, came out. The opening was about two feet long and two feet wide. It wasn't much. But it was enough to get the little boy out.

He lifted Shawn into the hole, instructing him, just as his sister had,

"You go find help! Don't come back until you bring somebody with something to break this door down with! OK?"

The kid, again, nodded vigorously. And within a moment, he was out.

By the time the boy was out of sight, the air around Marcus felt like it had depleted. He began to experience shortness of breath, coupled with an intense drawing within his belly. Beginning to feel like he was floating, he heard a voice behind him. . . It was low. The volume of a whisper. But it grew. . . gradually. . .

It had a dark humor about it,

"Funny thing about the *innocence* of children. . ."

The rasp grew menacingly,

". . . You never know when you can take them. . ."

It reverted back to a quieter tone, only this time as a growl,

". . . SERIOUSLY. . .!"

The malevolent speaker had taken form at Marcus's rear, and shoved his body into the door. With an abrupt convulsion, the teen was folded into the opening through which Shawn, was previously released. His shoulder blades met at the center of his vertebrae, with the touching of his elbows, and the interlocking of his reversed knuckles. He fell halfway back into the tomb; his knees clocked into the stone slab. He dangled, surging with fear only few have ever known. He wasn't ready to let go. He had to know who was fueling this adrenaline. . . He had to know what was able to break his athletic physique. Only then would he be ready to accept his fate. He turned his head as far backward as he could. Unfortunately, his mangling wouldn't allow much of any other contortion. But he caught a glimpse. Well. . . a "glimpse" was all there was, anyway. The light from the moon shone and within Marcus's path of sight was the bending, once again. Only, this time, he could make out a few details: such as the piercing blue eyes. Irises of cold sky, outlined with the white of death's skeletal face. It's arms were draped as a judge's robe. And the strangled hands, cuffed with this material, were decaying. . . seeming to be unfazed by the rot, the figure thrust it into the side of the teen's face.

The thing snarled again, protesting with a tisk as it pushed Marcus further through the hole,

"Nah ah ahh. . . Lovers in the dark. . . suffer no. . ."

It grunted from strain

". . . broken hearts!"

The teen's body fell to shambles on a nearby grave plot. He was twisted from his neck down, and completely destroyed.

Zira witnessed the night's horrific happenings, just sitting by the door. Her emotions swam; but she could never pull herself to intercede! All energy was wrung from her body and Spirit. As she moped, mourning the loss and unnerving torment of her friends, one form. . . among all the others in the chaos, and picking away at the sanity of the living. . . approached the young woman. She was stunned at his beauty. So much, in fact, that the closer he got, the less she saw of the world.

The being spoke in a tranquility with soft spaces between his words,

"I. . . am sorry. . . about what's happened to your friends."

The girl just gazed at the phenomenal apparition; now, unbothered by lament.

"Do you know. . ." he continued, ". . . who I am?"

She shook her head slowly.

"Well, then. . ." the creature chuckled, still as softly as he began, ". . . titles. . . aren't important. . ."

He stretched out his hand. The young woman, still enthralled and still unaware of who this creature was, obliged.

"I can take you. . . away. . . from all of this. . . Zira. Would you like that? Would. . . you want. . . to be free?"

The quiet, once frantic girl nodded now. She believed this "man" was her knight in shining armor. When in reality. . . the magnificent stranger was Death, and despite all of her previous imaginings from the stories describing him, she saw he was Good. Still, he had come to claim the souls of the young group.

Kim tried her best to pull Sasha to her senses, but failed. Realizing she could only save herself, she ran toward the gaping exit in the center of the door, ready to dive through. But Julian stood between her and her escape.

"The Witch" smiled as another demonic groaning mixed with her natural voice,

"Don't leave so soon, Kindergarten-Cup."

She snarled,

"You still haven't said 'GOODBYE', yet!"

The possessed Julian grabbed Kim by her slender throat. As Kim fought for a solemn breath, she felt her scalp stretch to its max. Her hair matted between the fingers of another, and they wrapped and twirled and gathered even more as they ascended to reach the top of her skull. A face peeked above her own. . . Chi-Chi now gazed down at the pale girl with glassy, hollow eyes, and he smiled a terrible toothy smile.

The tubby Latino, too, garbled with an evil ejection,

"We still haven't eaten, yet!"

A third presence emerged with a scrubbing sound.

A flash lit the room a bit brighter with the ignition of the lighter, and another face appeared. It was Miss Popularity, herself.

An equally domineering and maniacal essence was thrown from Sasha's gullet,

"Don't worry, brother. . ." she tugged Kim's loose locks,

"we'll remedy that quite. . ."

She lifted the flame to the girl's hair,

". . . quite. . . soon. . ."

Kim's waves combusted from the chemicals she'd used to get ready just hours before. Through the grip the babysitter had on her esophagus, she screamed. And screamed. And screamed. Until her breaths ceased to erupt, her body crisped upon the cold stone floor. Before long, and by some hell-wrought miracle, the entire tomb was in flames; from the bodies within, to the stain glass steeple, which finally shattered. Those left inside were consumed. . .

"Do you hear what I said? *'THEY WERE CONSUMED'* by the Guardians! And *FOR THE GODS!*

"Help finally arrived, but when they did, the Mausoleum was charred-black! Only skeletons remained! AND EVEN THOSE WERE REDUCED TO ASH WHEN MOVED IMPROPERLY!"

The narrator began losing his temperament on reality as he continued describing that horrific day,

"MARCUS LAY IN HIS OWN FLUIDS ON A GRAVE A FEW YARDS AWAY! AS IF HE TRIED CRAWLING TO SAFETY! AND NOW, *I* SEE THEM! AND THEY TELL ME THINGS! TERRIBLE THINGS! THEY WANT ME TO DIE TOO! AND I WANT TO DIE, DOC!! YOU HEAR ME?! IT'S THE ONLY WAY IT'LL END!"

Now, back in the present, the narrator's therapist sat across the desk,

"And you believe they're after you because you let your babysitter's friends and brother die?"

"MARCUS?!" the original speaker responded, "NO! No No! Marcus survived! He was the only other! He's in a wheelchair now. I'm the only one he's talked to since that night, fifteen years ago! All he can do is talk."

The narrator lowered his voice to a whisper, "And he told me what he saw. . ."

Again, he lifted his voice to speak normally,

"They're after me because they *were* going to kill me that night. They were going to vivisect me. And burn my organs while I watched." He gesticulated as if trying to show the doctor what exactly he meant,

"Then, *skin me* for new upholstery!"

His tone loudened one last time, "THEN. . . EAT ME! DOC! D'YA HEAR WHAT I JUST FUCKING SAID!? THEY WERE GOING TO FUCKING EAT ME!!!"

His therapist called through an intercom,

"NURSE! Please take young Shawn, here back to his room.

He looked back at his patient,

"Now Shawn, you're going to need to calm down. They weren't going to sacrifice you. Julian told you that. You're just suffering from Post-Traumatic Stress."

He leaned back into his chair to explain, "You saw your babysitter get hurt. That can cause some. . . unwanted thoughts to cross one's mind."

The nurse entered the doctor's office,

"Alright, sir." She spoke sweetly to the rattled Shawn, "Are we ready to go back to bed?"

The psychiatrist bid the man good evening with the final question,

"And. . . why are you still narrating?"

"I'm not!" he protested, "And no! I'm not going back to bed! They're in there! WAITING FOR ME!"

The nurse pulled Shawn into the foyer,

"Well, I'll make sure I get them out of your room so you can get some sleep."

His doctor called,

"And Nurse?"

She stopped to acknowledge.

"Up his dosage."

"Well. . . I'm awake now. Strapped to this bed. My shirt is being pulled up. I see them. They're about to do it! HELP! HEELLLLPPPP! NURSE! DOCTOR!!! HEEEEELLLLLLPPPPPP MMMMEEEEEE!!!"

Printed in the United States
By Bookmasters